A Nameless Place

Best wishes,

Pallavi Nally

A Nameless Place

Pallavi Hallur

Publisher

Cedar books

J-3/16, Daryaganj, New Delhi-110002
☎ 23276539, 23272783, 23272784 • *Fax:* 011-23260518
E-mail: info@pustakmahal.com • *Website:* www.pustakmahal.com

Sale Centre

- 10-B, Netaji Subhash Marg, Daryaganj, New Delhi-110002
  ☎ 23268292, 23268293, 23279900 • *Fax:* 011-23280567
  E-mail: rapidexdelhi@indiatimes.com

- **Hind Pustak Bhawan**
  6686, Khari Baoli, Delhi-110006
  ☎ 23944314, 23911979

Branches

Bengaluru: ☎ 080-22234025 • *Telefax:* 080-22240209
E-mail: pustak@airtelmail.in • pustak@sancharnet.in
Mumbai: ☎ 022-22010941, 022-22053387
E-mail: rapidex@bom5.vsnl.net.in
Patna: ☎ 0612-3294193 • *Telefax:* 0612-2302719
E-mail: rapidexptn@rediffmail.com
Hyderabad: *Telefax:* 040-24737290
E-mail: pustakmahalhyd@yahoo.co.in

© Author

Edition: 2009

ISBN 978-81-223-1093-1

Printed at : Param Offsetters, Okhla, New Delhi-110020

If you do not get it from yourself,
where will you go for it?

– Zen Proverb

This is dedicated to you,
my reader.

Acknowledgements

More than anyone else, I would like to thank my husband, Murali. He has supported all my inner quests and has encouraged me to create my own path, however unusual it may have seemed at times. I am constantly grateful for his love, patience and understanding.

I would also like to thank my sister, Apoorva, for sharing her inspiring thoughts with me, and my friend Michelle for encouraging me to write ever since we discussed our ideas with each other on a chilly autumn day in Cambridge five years ago.

There are many other people and circumstances that have contributed to the deep aspects of this simple story, but as with most deep things, they cannot be limited to names.

Thank you to the universe for revealing this story to me, and to all those unnamed angels that came to help me.

Introduction

This story is the result of a life-changing journey that began three years ago. The question of identity had always bothered me and I had always questioned the way people defined themselves. This had been an exclusively socio-political question for me; there was nothing spiritual about it. But all that began to change, very gradually, as my awareness entered a new realm, when I visited India.

Being originally Indian, I always had a connection with the subcontinent, but I had been torn away from it and had never experienced it as an adult until I decided to come back in 2006. Suddenly, I saw it from an entirely new perspective and it was a place where everything seemed to contradict. I observed hippies, *sadhus*, monks and nuns, all gathered in the same pursuit for transcendental knowledge. Alongside the deeply spiritual, other-worldly quest for eternal truth, I saw the very immediate struggle of poverty, violence, drought and hunger. Then there was the overtly materialistic life of the shops, the malls, glamour and riches. All these things grappled with each other in India's overcrowded spaces, spirituality, struggle and materialism in a tight embrace of love and hate.

It was only after living in India, being part of it and trying to understand its heart and soul that I began to see how its powerful forces work together in order to create something unique. This novel is the result of a few of the revelations that have come from being in India.

Prologue

The earthly smell of soil and water pervaded the thick, sombre air, making it convulse with a sultry grace. The monsoon was approaching once again the town of Dharna.

The road was smooth with the moisture of the recent rainfall and heavy globules of lucent water dripped lazily from the tin roofs of the small, worn shops that littered the roadside. Laxmi Gupta scanned the traffic before stepping onto the road. A wisp of hair blew across her face, obscuring her vision just as she was crossing the path of a speeding motorbike. Laxmi slowed down to brush away the dampened lock of hair and the biker honked his horn as he swerved around her, with only a few inches between them. Laxmi held her breath in horror until she was sure that the motorbike had passed. Death was a definite possibility in situations like this. India was full of death traps and the road was an obvious one. But India was also full of small mercies. Subhash was waiting for her in a café on the other side, so Laxmi didn't care much about the reckless traffic between them. Besides, death was not just a possibility – it was an inevitable fact which would enter everyone's realm of experience one day. Laxmi knew this as well as anyone. Her whole life had been moulded by the hands of death.

A restaurant in the side street had begun taking down its multi-coloured parasols now that the downpour had ended. The falling coloured stripes reminded Laxmi of the maypole ribbons that school children used to dance with when she was growing up in England.

She turned towards the corner and saw Subhash sitting outside Moonpeak Café, leafing through a soggy newspaper. He gave her a broad smile when he saw her approaching. The waiter brought out the drinks which Subhash had already ordered and Laxmi watched the steam rising from the cups between herself and Subhash. He began telling her about the article he had just read in the paper.

Laxmi listened contentedly to the sound of Subhash's soothing voice. She thought about her trip here and how it had answered a lot of the plaguing questions that she had carried around with her for years. India had confounded her, confused her, overwhelmed her and saved her. Sprawling, chaotic India had blessed her like a goddess holding up her palm with compassion, so that she was released by the ghosts of her past, mercifully unchained from the grip of self-hate and self-sabotaging tendencies into which she had unknowingly plunged. India had not given her a new identity, but it had revealed the identity that she had already been carrying, the one she could not see before, when she had been blinkered by grief and self-pity, embittered by fate's attempts to steal away everyone she had loved.

But India had also created complexity, a sweet and lingering dilemma brought on by the sudden experience of falling in love. In the process of forging her relationship with India, Laxmi had somehow fallen in love with the composed, unassuming man sitting across from her. Although Laxmi's feelings for Subhash were growing, neither of them had admitted that their relationship was anything more than friendship. She was supposed to go back to London soon, and Subhash would never be hers. He still hadn't confessed it to her, but she knew about his situation. She couldn't believe how much life had changed in eight fleeting months.

❏❏❏

Laxmi's Story

Chapter 1

I know the feeling of being trapped. So many times in the past, I would sit in the depths of a darkened room, wishing away the world outside, sometimes wishing away my life. Just before despair could set in fully, a sense of nothingness would overtake me, prompting me to continue with my useless existence for another day, if only because I didn't know any other way to live. But before that numbness could set in and save me from doing any real harm to myself, I would find myself confronted with a moment of anguish in which the futility of my whole existence would hit me like a wave, powerful and out of my control. The foundations of my life felt weak and worthless. Numerous questions would flood my mind. What is the purpose of my life? Why have I been born, just to breathe a few breaths and die, having achieved nothing worthwhile in the process? Who am I and what am I? If I end my life right now, will I get the release I crave or will there be another afterlife from which I can't escape?

I believed in the supernatural. I believed spirits could exist without a physical body. I had experienced paranormal incidents ever since I was a child: seeing apparitions of the dead, voices speaking to me in the darkness, my body becoming paralysed during sleep while my mind remained conscious. All of these things were dismissed as mental hallucinations and medical problems caused by depression or stress. I learned to ignore these inexplicable things, although they made me aware of something more than just the material world. It hardly made any difference to the way I felt. Despite all my strange experiences, I had never experienced the presence of a benevolent God. I had never known any kind of everlasting love. I had felt utterly alone for as long as I could remember.

I would hear the Christian preachers on the streets of London speak about having hope, shouting their messages with passion as crowds of busy Londoners walked past without even glancing in their direction. Hope… it sounded like a beautiful word, like an ointment an injured person could rub on his or her wounds, which could give her strength to walk a little further towards some heavenly door. I admired people who could fool themselves into a lifetime of hope.

Despite my dissatisfaction with life, I couldn't say I ever had a strong hope that something better was possible, although I had plenty of regrets. Occasionally, I would long for a fresh start, the chance to create myself anew, but I never had the courage to actually change anything. With change, there is always a risk that things will only become worse. At the age of twenty-six, I had become extremely cynical very fast.

But then, quite recently, something strange happened to me and I had an inkling of what it might feel like to have hope, enough hope to allow me to become courageous. I saw a possibility for myself being content and it came from the realisation that I had lost something important to me, which I might be able to find again. Once this realisation dawned on me, once hope offered her ointment and her promise, then gathering the courage to change my life did not take much time.

I was able to take the first step. I felt ready to take the risk of losing everything I had because whatever I had felt suddenly meaningless. All I had was a degree of security in the form of a job, a flat, and a daily routine, but I no longer wanted a security which kept me trapped in depression. None of my family members or acquaintances needed me in their lives, so I wasn't afraid to be walking out on anyone.

My life was like a jigsaw puzzle with a vital piece missing from it and something had inspired me to think that I could find that missing piece again. Based on this hope, I made the decision to go on this journey.

I might not find what I am looking for from this, but I have decided to take a chance. A thick fog of uncertainty lies ahead, with the risk of tripping or falling along the way, but even a fall on this path would be better than the life I was leading before, because at least I would know for sure that I had tried.

So here I am. The plane is rising higher into the pale blue sky. I am making a journey in search of something intangible. It sounds reckless, naïve and irrational to search for something which has no physical substance, something which exists only as an idea. But it's an idea that shapes worlds, societies and cultures. It gives people the conviction to know themselves and perhaps it will do the same for me.

London fades away beneath me, its suburban greenery and labyrinthine inner-city blur into patches of colour. Ghostly clouds move past my window, shrouding my view of the place I am leaving. The place I am going to will be so different and I must prepare myself. I chose to make this trip because I wanted to escape that darkened room. I cannot now shy away from the light, however uncomfortable it might be to put myself under the scrutiny of an unknown world. I am going to a place which was once so familiar but has now become so alien to me that I really don't know what to expect from it. But I'm ready to go back.

❏❏❏

Chapter 2

As I sit here in the plane, I can't help thinking back to that surreal day when I had decided to make this journey to return to India, my motherland. It was on a dull grey Monday morning. I had woken up with that same desperate sense of emptiness, which reverberated all around my empty flat. Of course, it wasn't completely empty because I was there, but somehow I didn't think I was occupying any space. I had turned on the TV to create some sound, the illusion of company. I remember word for word what the psychologist on the morning talk show had been saying...

"The fact that you exist does not make you special," Dr Jones, the psychologist on the therapy panel, had been stating emphatically. "It's the way in which you recognise your existence that makes the difference between leading a fulfilling life or a meaningless one. But the recognition of who you are – your identity, you could say – has to be based on truth and not on lies that you've told yourself, because somewhere in your subconscious mind, you already know everything about yourself. This subconscious knowledge has to filter into your conscious mind. If you know yourself consciously, if you understand your roots, your past, your strengths and weaknesses, then you can heal yourself and resolve your issues instead of trying to run away from them. You can give more to others and find a real sense of meaning in being alive."

The row of drug addicts and alcoholics on the stage stared blankly at the psychologist, some of them nodding morosely. The talk show host promised all of them a free counselling session with Dr Jones after the show. After listening sceptically for a few minutes, I reached for the remote control and switched off the television.

The words of the psychologist had made me feel irritated, with their idealistic notions of 'truth' and 'identity'. The psychologist had also reminded me of the frustrating recurring dream that I had been having for the past five years, in which an old man would repeatedly ask me to explain who I was, whilst my mouth was gagged so

I could not speak. That day, like every other day of my adult life, I could feel no real sense of identity.

I was beginning to realise that my lack of identity had corroded all of my adult relationships. I only had one friend from my school days whom I could talk openly to. Although I had had many short-term relationships, none of them had lasted very long. I had cared little about most of my past relationships with men, as I didn't think they could ever truly satisfy me, but the pain of one particular break-up had still not healed. The only time that I had been in love, I had lost that love because of my inability to open up fully to another person. I had been thinking a lot about Adam that day, wondering why things had gone wrong between us, as I got myself ready for another day.

I had been working in an inner-city bookstore for three years. It was here that I had met Adam for the first time, the one man whom I'd loved. I had not heard from him at all since he left, and I had lost count of how many weeks it had been since the break-up.

It had been a painful relationship. He had opened himself to me whole-heartedly and I had been unable to do the same for him. He had introduced me to his family, taken me out to meet his friends, shown me the place where he'd grown up. I had been enthusiastic and interested in everything he revealed to me, but I had kept myself quite distant when it came to talking about my family.

Adam had thought that I was afraid to be in a mixed race relationship and felt ashamed about introducing him to the people I cared about, although I had told him time and again that this was not the case, that I simply wasn't very close to anyone. But that did not explain why I couldn't even talk to him about what had happened in my past, why I never mentioned my parents or my childhood.

Eventually, he had become tired of pushing me to speak about my feelings, my childhood, my parents, my memories. He had described these as 'the things that make us who we are'. I had agreed, but I still could not open up emotionally.

Only one of my school friends, Maria, knew about my past and I couldn't recreate that childish openness with anyone in my adulthood. With Adam, I had tried to think of something that would sound acceptable, but every memory or emotion I had was tainted with a feeling of loss, and when it came to forming a picture that could be shared, my mind would very often turn against me. All I could remember were shadows.

I refused to immortalise those shadows by showing them to Adam and making them a part of our relationship. But then there was no relationship left, because the shadows were all I had. So Adam gave up and left.

Why do life stories always begin at birth, even though we have no control over where we are born or to whom? Why do people judge us on something completely out of our control? I had wanted my story to begin afresh with my first encounter with Adam, which was still crystal clear in my mind.

I had been stacking books in the Reference area of the bookshop – a mundane activity which I couldn't wait to be freed from so that I could move onto the New Fiction stock. It was then that I had noticed a man with dark brown hair walking towards me. He was attractive, but I had not properly acknowledged his appeal at that point. Then he stopped me and I could see the warmth in his smile. He looked at me for a moment but I turned away from his glance. He asked if I could recommend an anthology of poetry as a birthday present for his mother. I took him to the Poetry shelf and pulled out an anthology called *Poem for the Day*.

"With this," I suggested, "you could show your mother that she's special every day, not just on her birthday."

"Well," Adam had mused, "I like that idea. Are you always so good at choosing gifts for people?" His eyes reflected a relaxed tenderness which I found compelling; it made me think of carefree summer days when, for a while, there was nothing to worry about except the freshly cut grass and the daisies growing in the fields. I laughed as I passed the book into his hands, wondering why he seemed so interested in me. In his typically open-hearted manner, he asked me out then and there.

And that's how it had started, our five-month relationship of highs and lows. I had never felt so drawn to anyone as I felt towards Adam. It was as though he represented everything I thought a human being should be: kind, confident, open and loving. I fell in love for the first time and Adam seemed drawn to me too, but we could not make it work – and it was because of me.

I dismissed those memories from my mind as I continued walking towards the tube station on that strange day. It was a continuous effort to stop myself from remembering him. I would never be with Adam again and I had to come to terms with that. I didn't have the energy and the ability to fight for that relationship. Adam said that he thought I was actually afraid of being happy. I neither argued with him nor agreed with him, but I understood what he was trying to say. I kept my distance from things that I felt could never really last, like happiness or love.

That day, I was in a perpetual daze, and at lunchtime, as I sat down on a bench in Regent's Park, the words of the psychologist came back to me. He had spoken of 'the real truth of who you are'. I knew that my name was Laxmi Gupta, that I was twenty-six years old and worked in a bookshop, but I had no sense of self beyond these facts. For several minutes I sat completely motionless, aside from any breathing, beating and blinking. I observed the movement around me as a complete outsider to the scene. I could hear the sound of traffic speeding past as the leaves fell to the ground.

Everything around me was moving and changing. People were walking along the leaf-strewn pathways: couples holding hands, parents holding their children, talking amongst themselves in various accents and languages. In the face of London's variety, I could see that love was a universal thing. I observed the array of light and colour that shone from people's eyes; they barely acknowledged anyone outside of their own circles and they looked happy and satisfied with themselves.

That's when I realised that these people had a particular kind of self-recognition which I lacked: they had a sense of community, as if they knew where they belonged, whom they belonged to. I had never known that feeling of certainty. These people were not all locals, but they knew they belonged either there in London or somewhere else.

Then it occurred to me that this was the reason why I feel so unsure of myself. I am neither British nor Indian, and I cannot identify with that third category which combines both of these cultures whilst somehow denying each. No one ever taught me about my original background, my heritage, my roots. I could see why my life felt like a sham – there was no cultural identity available for me to build upon, especially since I had lost my parents.

When this realisation began to dawn on me – that this was the reason for all my problems with relationships, with my lack of self-certainty and my dissatisfaction with life – that's when I began feeling something similar to hope. I felt that maybe I could fix or replace what had been lost.

Just then, I remembered that I did have a concrete cultural identity to begin with, but it had been neglected over the years. I think identity is something that needs to be preserved, like history, otherwise a part of who we are will be lost for ever. Maybe I needed to make more effort to acquaint myself with my cultural identity; maybe doing this could help me come to terms with my past, to become sure of myself, to open up to another human being. That was the day I seriously began to think about India and my roots.

I was born in a small Indian town and had been raised there until I was almost seven years old. My birth town, Dharna, had been my first home and I had felt rooted there as a child; there was nothing to contest my identity at that time. I have only blurry recollections of my birthplace, but a few scenes flash through my mind sometimes.

The memory that surfaced that day in the park was of a garden where I am watching the rain fall onto bright banana leaves. It is my grandmother's garden, and I am four years old in this scene. My grandmother's garden is wild and exotic, full of fragrance and colour. One particular plant is special to me because its colour is exquisite: its leaves are of the deepest, darkest green, speckled with light pink pigments that shine from the moisture of the rain drops. I held that image in my mind as I sat there in Regent's Park and I was touched by its simplicity. I remembered knowing myself then, feeling rooted like that small plant.

That was the moment when I decided to go back to India, to finally visit the country where I was born and where my parents had died.

❏❏❏

Chapter 3

That evening when I got home from work, I rang my only friend, Maria, to tell her about my decision. She had recently become very busy with her husband and newborn baby, but she wanted to talk to me about my plan. She only lived a few miles out of the city, so we agreed to meet at my flat for dinner the next day.

I was always grateful for Maria's company whenever she visited. She understood me well and I had missed her a lot since we left school to follow our separate paths.

Maria had found out about my parents' death on my very first day at our boarding school. She had overheard a conversation between the Headmistress and my aunt and uncle, which had taken place in the school corridor whilst the Headmistress was showing us around the school. Maria had been on one of her frequent trips to the washroom at the time, standing behind a giant Christmas tree, metres away from us.

In the conversation, my uncle had explained my situation quite directly to the Headmistress. He told her that I had just come from India, that I had lost my parents in a road accident when I was only two, and had been looked after by my paternal grandmother in a small Indian town called Dharna since then.

He also explained how my grandmother had been closest to me, but that she had recently passed away, so they had brought me to England with them because there was no other family member who had the means to look after me. I only had one other aunt, who had five of her own children to take care of.

Maria had been shocked by the story, although she, like me, was only seven years old at the time. She said that was the reason why she had stared at me so much during our first class together. She couldn't imagine someone's parents being dead: everyone she knew had a mother and a father. Being the only brown person in the class, I had hardly noticed her stares amongst all the others.

On my first day at the English Boarding School where I'd stay for the next ten years, Maria had come over to sit with me and had taken the first step towards friendship. That bond forged in childhood was still intact. It was the only relationship that had remained unscathed by my introversion. Somehow, Maria understood me even when I couldn't speak about things.

Perhaps it was because we had grown through a language barrier, as I couldn't speak much English when we first became friends. I had just come from a small town in India, where everyone around me used to speak to me in Hindi. Maria would sometimes marvel at the way children pick up languages by reminding me how little English I used to know and how quickly I became fluent.

The doorbell chimed loudly and I opened the front door. Maria shook the water out of her umbrella and stepped into the flat.

She looked oddly contrasted to the rain drizzling in streams outside. She was wearing a bright yellow summer dress with winding green leaf-patterns on it.

"Aren't you feeling a bit cold wearing that?" I asked her.

"Not at all," she answered with a nonchalant smile. "I've always been a warm-blooded type."

I laughed and led her into the kitchen. It was comforting to be in Maria's company. She exuded an air of confidence that was infectious, a bit like Adam. Her hazel eyes focused on the bags I had taken out of the cupboard, ready to be packed for my trip to India.

"So, you're actually going?" she asked incredulously. "This isn't just another fantasy?"

Maria and I had shared a fair few fantasies about the future, which included travelling the world and visiting places of miraculous beauty, getting away from the gloom of the old school library and the grey rain streaking its large windows. But the idea of going back to India was far from a fantasy for me.

"This is for real, Maria," I told her. "I have to find my roots, find out about my parents."

Maria nodded. I saw sadness in her eyes as she said softly, "I guess you have to do it, otherwise you'll never feel certain of who you are."

I nodded and there was a moment's silence. Then Maria looked straight at me and added, "But I know who you are."

I could tell what was coming next. Maria's family belonged to the Church of England like most other English families; they were liberal Protestants. Although most of her family members were not particularly religious, the impact of going to a highly old-fashioned Catholic Boarding School had caused Maria to think deeply about which aspects of her religion she really believed in.

Over the years, Maria had become a devout Christian, but unlike either her family or our Catholic school teachers, Maria had developed very unconventional views about Christianity. Throughout our teenage years, I had seen her honing her ideas about her religion, first rejecting the casual rituals practised by her family during Easter and Christmas, and then challenging the beliefs our teachers preached to us in our morning assemblies.

She began reading numerous books by scholars, religious leaders and psychics. Then, one day, she proclaimed, "Jesus can't save us from our sins. In fact, I don't think he was immaculately conceived or that he died after the crucifixion. Lots of people agree that he may have become unconscious and then woken up later."

"Careful, Maria," I'd said nervously. "Some people around here would want to hang you for saying things like that."

Many of our teachers were very religious, occasionally reminding us that accepting Jesus meant a reward of eternal life in heaven, and hinting that rejecting him meant an afterlife in hell. They were particularly interested in enlightening me about Christianity, as I was the only Hindu in my school in those years. But Maria had not meant to reject Jesus by her controversial statements, as I later realised.

"Oh, c'mon," Maria had protested, "we're moving towards the twenty-first century. We're all entitled to have different views. I actually believe more in what

Jesus taught now than I ever did before, but I think he was just a man with a special connection with God, not God himself. But do you know why I think he was still amazing, despite not being everything the *Bible* says?"

"Why?" I asked. "I mean, I know he healed the sick and that he was punished without committing any crime."

"Yes, Laxmi," Maria carried on, "but the most amazing thing about him was that he changed the way people thought about God. Up until then, people believed that God was ruthless and selfish; they believed in 'an eye for an eye' and all that. He gave people a new perspective. And that's what I respect."

I was expecting a similar kind of lecture from Maria that evening when she told me that she 'knew' who I was. As we began eating, she touched the silver cross chained around her neck and said, "I'm not going to try and brainwash you into my belief system. I know who you are because I know what kind of person you are and you know it too, but you just don't realise it yet. Your cultural background doesn't define your soul, Laxmi. God doesn't have a race or a culture and we're all His children."

"Maria," I argued, "I know you believe in these universal things, but by and large, the world doesn't agree with you. Religion doesn't bring people together, it just divides people. Everyone I've known, apart from you, has expected me to know myself through my cultural background. And I agree with them that it's important, otherwise, why would I be feeling so confused?"

"Because you've let their values influence you," Maria replied patiently. "You know I don't care about religious groups. I know it is mainly about power and division. I believe in the spirit, and the spirit does transcend your name, nationality, background, family and everything else in the material world."

"Right," I had said dismissively, "but we have to live in the material world, don't we?"

Maria smiled and nodded. I'd had the final say but I didn't feel any sense of victory. Maria had a conviction in what she was saying and I couldn't understand it at all. We soon changed the subject to more practical matters about my trip.

After Maria left that night, I began packing some of my clothes and typed up a resignation letter for work. I made a list of things I would have to organise, such as my finances, plane tickets, and possibly a work placement for the time I would be in India. I decided to call my aunt and uncle the next day to tell them about my trip.

❑❑❑

Chapter 4

I have noticed that people often hold onto something because it is familiar – it may be a place, a job or even a relationship. But just because it is familiar and safe doesn't make it satisfying or fulfilling. I had suddenly reached the point where I knew I had to leave the lifestyle I had known since I was a child.

Sitting here in the plane, so many unanswered questions are racing through my mind. Except for a couple of black-and-white wedding photos, I don't really know what my parents were like and I barely remember my grandmother's house. I had never been close enough to my aunt and uncle to discuss these things with them.

Vijay Uncle and Bhavna Auntie did not have any children of their own. I think they had liked the idea of adopting a little girl when they first brought me to the UK, but when they faced the actual prospect of raising me, they must have realised it was too time-consuming for their demanding careers. At least this is what I'd gathered from their distant demeanour and the choice to send me to a boarding school.

Vijay Uncle had been working as a lawyer in a well-reputed firm for many years and Bhavna Auntie was a doctor in the UK's National Health Service. They were a very ambitious, self-motivated couple whose desire to reach the top of their professions left little time for any family bonding.

But they had always been good to me and I was grateful to them for supporting me after my grandmother's death, even though our relationship had remained quite formal over the years. I don't think they had approved of my choice of studying Linguistics at university or of the fact that I had quit three different office jobs and was now working at a bookstore.

Although they were emotionally distant, from each other as well as from me, Vijay Uncle and Bhavna Auntie were very good with practical things; they had a lot of connections. When I told them I wanted to get some sort of work placement during my stay in India, they used their contacts to find something for me.

They were a little surprised that I wanted to go back to India, as I hadn't been there a single time since my grandmother's death. I couldn't remember all the people I had known as a child in Dharna, but my aunt and uncle still had links with people in their native town, which they used to get me a teaching job for the year. I agreed to take the position because I didn't have much choice, although the thought of teaching made me feel a little nervous.

Vijay Uncle informed me that there was a small school in Dharna which was happy to take an English teacher and that they would even pay me a basic salary. He seemed pleased that I would be doing something more professional at last. The old neighbour who had told my uncle about this possibility had known my grandmother. This neighbour, Mr Chakram, was a landlord who said he had a suitable place for me to stay during my time in Dharna. He told my uncle over the phone that he remembered me well and had been very fond of me when I was a child. Sadly, I could not recall him at all.

I took down the details of the school and its Headmaster, Mr Agarwal, as well as the name and address of the old neighbour, Mr Chakram. The practical details had been fixed. All I had left to do was to book my flight to Delhi, where Vijay Uncle's sister lived, and to find out about trains from Delhi to Dharna, the small hill-station where my parents had lived and where I would be spending the most part of a year.

Vijay Uncle had advised me to stay with his sister instead of booking a hotel for my time in Delhi and I had reluctantly consented. None of my relatives had been in touch with me over the years and I didn't want to force a feeling of informality. But I told myself that the whole point of this journey was to find out about my cultural background, so everyone who had a link to that background could help me know more about it.

❑❑❑

Chapter 5

We are rapidly climbing the skies. This is a territory that cannot be marked by houses, shops or any other symbols of humanity. It is blank, pure and free. I feel free within its dimensions, as dependent as I may be on the Boeing 747 as it moves blanketed by clouds. The man sitting next to me has introduced himself as Rajiv. He seems very pleasant and also very excited to be going to Delhi.

I cannot sleep during the long flight. Instead, I think about India, that massive, sprawling country. My own memories of it are lacking but I have seen so many images of India in the British media over the years. They usually show the country's poverty: children born into the dust of its streets, playing cricket in torn clothes or women in colourful *saris*, labouring for daily wages.

Although India is my birthplace, I know I could not live there permanently anymore. I am relying on it to give me a sense of understanding so that I can come and settle back in London with a secure identity. It may sound childish to need one place to give you an identity and another to give you a home, but that's the paradox my life has now become.

The realities I have become accustomed to would be impossible to recreate in India, where I am doubtful of the language, the work environment and the living habits. All I want is the kind of certainty I saw in those people in Regent's Park – they were from different places but had adjusted to living in London and seemed secure in themselves.

Maybe I am being presumptuous by thinking that the people walking through the park that day had never questioned their own identities. Maybe everyone questions their identity, even if they have lived in the same town their whole lives, with their parents, grandparents, aunts, uncles, and a whole community around them. Maybe everyone goes through an identity crisis and eventually gets over it like it's a phase, similar to getting one's body pierced or tattooed in an attempt to be someone you are not, someone you will eventually stop trying to be once you become comfortable in your own skin. Maybe most people grow out of identity crises like they grow out of smoking pot or dying their hair blue. It doesn't stop them from finding someone to love, it doesn't stop them from opening up to another person or feeling like their life has a purpose.

I plug in my headphones and flick through the channels on the miniature television screen in front of me. Rajiv is happily watching a Bollywood film of high drama, while I debate whether to go for the recent British hit or try to practise my Hindi by watching the Bollywood films. I eventually decide on neither and start reading the book I brought with me, *Travels on My Elephant*.

When the stewardess brings over the meals, I echo Rajiv's choice for the vegetarian option. Rajiv asks me if I chose to become vegetarian or whether it's part of my religion. I tell him that it's not because of religion; I just don't like the idea of meat.

We begin talking about the validity of vegetarianism. Eventually he moves onto telling me about his life in the UK. He is a doctor, like my aunt, and has been working in the National Health Service for the past year. As he describes his life in a foreign land, I can tell from the tone of his voice the kind of alienation and loneliness he feels in being far away from home. He is going back to India for a two-week holiday.

His tone cheers up dramatically when he switches to telling me about his hometown, his family and friends. I find engaging with him, a perfect stranger, easier than

I thought I would, and I begin asking him about his choice to go to the UK in the first place.

"Why not stay at home if that's where you really want to be?" I ask him.

He looks at me with a dry smile as if to forgive my lack of understanding. His explanation is that he wants to make a better life for himself and his family. He has the same ambitious streak as my aunt and uncle.

I think to myself about what 'better' really means – can economic prosperity fill the hole of yearning for a place you can call home? But I have not known any real poverty, so who am I to judge Rajiv's choices? I quietly eat a spoonful of the mango dessert, and its familiar flavour fills my mouth. I can taste India approaching.

Rajiv eventually asks me if I am married and hints that his parents are looking for a wife for him. I feel glad for him that he will soon have a companion in a foreign country. Being in the UK is not alienating for me in the same way it is for most first-generation immigrants. I have got used to the customs and colloquialisms, picking up the language and habits without question the way most children do when they are taken abroad. I know it must have been hard at the start, although I can barely remember that time.

Rajiv's sense of self is so firmly rooted in India that it will probably take a lifetime for him to adapt fully to another culture. I can just imagine his wife arriving in his flat, dressed like a new bride with vermilion in her hair and bangles on her wrists, cooking traditional meals in the kitchen and waiting for Rajiv to come home after spending days and nights on duty. It will probably be harder for her than it is for him.

Like so many Indian couples, they may have children that grow up being foreign to them, unable to carry forward the tradition that their environment has erased all traces of. But their parents will be there to impart the knowledge necessary to make them understand their roots and that might be enough for them to form a sense of identity, however fragile and conflicting it may be.

As if to correct the direction of my thoughts, Rajiv suddenly says, "I will not stay in the UK for long. India is opening up many opportunities now and many people are going back."

I have recently heard a lot about this new trend of Indians migrating back to the motherland, and even of foreigners seizing work opportunities in India. Vijay Uncle has mentioned a couple of his colleagues who have left the UK for jobs in India.

"Has it really developed so much?" I ask Rajiv, thinking about the poverty-stricken images that my mind associates with my birthplace.

"Oh yes," Rajiv says passionately. "You can get anything and everything, especially in the big cities like Delhi. Cappuccino, Frappacino, Swiss chocolate, you name it. And in the malls, you won't believe you're actually still in India because they're so westernised. A lot of my friends working in the field of IT have more luxurious lives than I do in the UK!"

"Really?" I ask. "I haven't been there for so long – has it really changed that much?"

I can't hide my surprise. The picture I have formed of India over the years does not include malls or cafés; it includes dusty roads with cows contending with traffic and vegetable sellers standing on the street corners.

"Yes, yes, it's very good," Rajiv continues. "But please do not expect to see change everywhere. The roads are still bad and there are still water and electricity problems. The villagers are still uneducated and many farmers still use bullock carts. This change has only happened on one level of society."

"Oh, right," I say with a nod. I notice that Rajiv looks a little worried that he's ruined the impressive image of India he'd previously shared with me, so I quickly add, "I don't know what to expect, but whatever it is, I'll have to deal with it."

"Don't worry, Miss Laxmi," Rajiv assures me, "I am certain that India is on the way. You will feel quite comfortable."

❏❏❏

Chapter 6

The hours pass by quietly as the sky changes from light to dark. Even if I look down through the rounded windows, I cannot make out the earth below. I finally fall into a light sleep and am suddenly awoken by turbulence. The pilot announces that we are shortly to arrive in Delhi, but that our landing at Indira Gandhi International Airport may be delayed while we wait for a runway to be cleared for us.

I look at the screen mapping our journey and notice after some minutes that we are hovering in circles above Delhi, waiting for permission to land. I was naïve to think that the empty skies were a free territory: the politics on land affect the air, the water and even the skies. The aeroplanes themselves represent nations and territories.

The airline I am flying with is Italian and therefore all its communications are in Italian, which is then translated into English. The fact that English translations are so necessary for everyone makes me wonder about the strange relationship the world now has with the English language. Very few native English speakers feel the need to learn any other language, whilst people all over the world strive to learn English as a way to improve their prospects in the world.

I remember when I had just arrived in England from India and could barley understand a word of English. The limitation of not being able to understand and express is a feeling I can still remember. In the beginning when I started at boarding school, I tried to speak to the other girls in Hindi, but they would stare back at me blankly, looking at me like I was absurd.

There was one school incident that was particularly frustrating. We had to write a story about what we had done over the weekend. I wanted to say that I had received an exciting parcel – a new pair of shoes – as a gift from my aunt, but the English for 'shoes' was absent from my vocabulary. I could only think of the Hindi word, *joota*, which my grandmother had always used when she was chiding me for running outside without wearing any shoes or slippers: "*Phir se joota chappal pahane bina bahaar chali gayi!*" she would tut ("Again you went out without wearing any shoes or slippers!").

So, remembering my Hindi, I helplessly tried using this Hindi word with my class teacher and asked her for its English equivalent. The teacher was understandably confused and this confusion began to get more and more tiring as I kept repeating myself in Hindi. Finally, I pointed at my shoes and she gave me a word. I accepted it gratefully.

Later, when my story was read out to the class along with everybody else's stories, the other children looked at me as if I'd written something offensive. I couldn't understand my own story, so I presumed that the word the teacher had given me must have been the wrong one.

To this day, I still don't know what that word was, but I can't forget the feeling of being embarrassingly misunderstood. That day the group of girls I used to play with in the school yard began avoiding me and I couldn't ask them why my story had bothered them. My story must have appeared ridiculous to them, even though the teacher had accepted it as a good attempt.

I snap back into the present moment as I hear the thud and screech of the aeroplane's wheels on the runway. We have finally landed in India.

As I descend the stairs from the plane, I realise that the journey is still not over. There are four rickety buses waiting outside the plane, preparing to take passengers up to the airport's arrival point. The exhaust fumes fill the dense humid air, while the paint on the buses continues to peel helplessly, making feeble attempts to cover their metallic nakedness.

As we cram into the second bus, a middle-aged businessman shakes his head smilingly and says with some sarcasm, "Welcome to India". Twenty minutes later, after much stopping and restarting, the bus pulls up in front of the arrival point. There is a groan of relief from the passengers, and an impatient scramble to get off the bus. Some Indians decide to show their learned foreign patience by trying to queue quietly and I decide to wait around with them until the crowd clears.

Queuing at immigration is easier than I'd anticipated and I soon find myself entering the baggage claim area, where there are five different turning belts displaying the luggage brought down from the planes. But there is havoc and confusion because we can see no indication of which belt corresponds to which flight.

I ask a man collecting his bag whether he has any idea about the luggage from my flight. He shrugs unknowingly and points to his bags, "These have come from the Amsterdam plane," he tells me. Well, that eliminates one out of the five belts. I decide to ask an Indian airport assistant who is roaming the area. I swallow my hesitation to speak in Hindi, realising that this is my first opportunity to practise my much neglected mother-tongue. I enunciate carefully and, thankfully, the airport assistant understands me and directs me to belt two.

While I am waiting for my single trolley-case to appear, a middle-aged woman approaches me cheerfully. She is petite and of Indian origin, wearing trousers and thin-rimmed spectacles. Looking at the passport in my hands, she says, "So, you've come from the UK? I am from Trinidad."

"Um, yes," I reply, not knowing what more to say about my passport. She continues, "Were you born in the UK? I was born in Trinidad. I'm just here to visit my sister. Are you here on a holiday too?"

No, I think to myself. *I wish it were that simple.* Out loud I say, "Actually, I was born in India. I have lived in the UK since I was seven and I've come back to visit."

She accepts this explanation with a mild hint of surprise. I feel a little guilty for denying my British nationality. After all, I studied there, worked there and lived there. I am grateful to the place that became my solitary refuge and it will always be special to me. It's just that my roots are not there and I have been reminded of that fact many times. I'm hoping that I might find those lost roots somewhere here in India, so that I can take the essence of that identity back with me. All I ask of India is to grant me the security I need to live freely in England, which is the place I now understand but where I've never felt fully accepted.

I collect my bag and step through the green channel. I feel anxious as I search for my aunt in the throngs of brown faces waiting outside the airport – I don't know if I'll recognise her.

Soon enough, I spot a placard with my name written on it, held up by a withered but dignified-looking old man in a white cotton *kurta*. I walk towards him, trying to dodge people and luggage. He smiles amiably and says in good English, "*Namaste* madam, your Archana Auntie has sent me to collect you. I am the driver."

He leads me to a silvery green car, marked with the Tata Indigo logo, and somehow we squeeze out of the mesh of cars, taxis and auto rickshaws. The open road takes on an eerie appearance in the dusky light. It is around seven pm in New Delhi.

After a long and a dusty drive, we pull into a residential passage in a leafy suburb. The driver takes out my bag and gestures towards the ground floor apartment. I cautiously ring the doorbell.

A vaguely familiar-looking woman steps out with an uncertain smile. She is in her late fifties, with grey hair wrapped into a bun at the nape of her neck. Her sari is elegantly tied, with pale blue patterns on a crisp white cotton that lends the woman an air of brightness and serenity. This is Archana Auntie, my father's elder sister, and I can already see her resemblance to Vijay Uncle in England.

She gives me a hug which I feel awkwardly unprepared for. Then I am led through her wide courtyard, which has a small tree in the centre and various plants lined in neat pots around the edges.

The evening is hot and sticky, unlike the autumn chill I have been used to. My aunt shows me around her house, which is very neat and simply decorated. I have a wash with refreshingly cool water and then come to sit at the dining table, where some food has been laid out for us by the maid.

My aunt serves me some rice with *dal,* a simple lentil dish, with fried okra on the side. The food is not very spicy but it tastes wholesome and delicious. It reminds me of some distant time when eight-minute pastas and boiled carrots did not form part of my daily diet.

My aunt begins to ask me about England and how I've been. She has never visited the UK, although she recently travelled to America because her son, my cousin whom I've never met, is a doctor there. I tell her that Bhavna Auntie and Vijay Uncle are well in England. She seems pleased to hear about her younger brother and sister-in-law. She is the eldest of three children; my father was the youngest.

I feel very awkward, although Archana Auntie does not seem to sense this and she looks quite relaxed and comfortable in her environment. She is kind and courteous, but we have barely spent any time together and feigning closeness requires effort for me. I can't see any memory of my grandmother in her face and I assume she must have got her sharp, lean appearance from my grandfather, who died years before I was born. My grandmother, whom I was so attached to, was small and sturdy with soft features.

Thankfully, the meal is soon over and my aunt tells me to rest in the guest bedroom. I thank her for the meal and she laughs at my politeness, which I think she sees as formality instead of as a sign of respect. I retire to the bedroom and as I fall onto the bed, after many months I feel I will have a good night's sleep without any dreams or questions or uncertainties plaguing me. I don't even care to check if the door is locked tonight, the way I usually do at least three or four times each night at the flat in London. I don't know where this restful sensation has come from – perhaps from the tiredness of a long journey or the delicate humming of the ceiling fan. I spray some mosquito repellent on my arms and switch off the light.

❏❏❏

Chapter 7

It must be very early but already the doorbell has started to ring and vegetable sellers have started calling out in the street with a yodelling declaration of their goods. I could sleep on for hours, but this is not my own place, so I make myself get up. I rinse my eyes in the adjoining bathroom and walk towards the dining room. My aunt is having tea at the table whilst supervising the maid. She is neatly dressed in a pink and white sari. I admire the fact that she is not subscribing to the rigid customs of Hindu widowhood by wearing white all the time.

"Good morning, my dear," she says to me endearingly.

"Good morning," I respond with a smile.

She looks me up and down as if acknowledging me fully for the first time since I arrived. "You've turned out very well, though perhaps a bit too thin. But fine features, just like your mother. Here, have breakfast."

I gratefully pour myself a cup of tea and take a *paratha*, a flat sundry made from flour and oil. I look through the Delhi paper on the dining table, which is filled with as much Bollywood gossip as it is with current affairs. So far, Rajiv was right – I do feel reasonably comfortable here in the sheltered environment of the suburbs. Sooner or later, though, I'll have to venture out into the overcrowded city.

* * *

After breakfast, my aunt tells me that the driver is available to take me out, and three hours later, I am in one of Delhi's recently built 'malls'. As Rajiv had described, there are plenty of chic shops selling globally-known brands of food and cosmetics. Small Indian adjustments have been made to the creams and toiletries, like the fact that instead of skin tanning lotions, here they display a multitude of skin whitening creams. I laugh to myself, wondering why, at least in the realm of skin colour, people want to be the opposite of what they are. It seems to me that perceptions of beauty are strongly influenced by economics.

In the West, tanned skin now represents health and prosperity, while in India, light skin shows that a person can afford to shelter themselves from labouring in the harsh sun, much like in Victorian England when it was stylish for women to be plump and 'lily white'. Maria once told me that societies use oppositions to try and define themselves, to set judgements and values, like wrong and right, thin and fat, black and white. We measure ourselves in relative terms and that's why we're never happy.

From the mall balcony I notice a long line of slums across the road. I see a woman sitting in a ragged hut with her baby, darkened by the sun's blaze, emaciated and worn out with labour. Her face strikes me as tremendously beautiful, with elegantly shaped and perfectly proportioned features. Yet, it seems that no one here would notice her beauty because she is carrying the unpleasantness of poverty with her. I turn back into the mall area, which is full of commotion and bustle, a different world from the slums across the street.

I go into a modern bookshop-cum-café and order myself a café latte. Upper middle-class Indians dressed in western clothes and speaking in English are scattered around the room, with a few tourists and travellers sitting in the corner. I have tried to gel with the surroundings as much as possible by wearing a *salwar kameez* but I don't think it would have mattered to anyone sitting in here, as most of them are wearing jeans and skirts. With my Indian-looking face, no one can tell I am from abroad. They would only find out if they spoke to me for some minutes and heard the cracks in my Hindi.

When the waiter brings over my latte, I thank him and ask for the menu, enunciating a little too much so that he understands my accent. The latte is creamy and tastes like real Italian coffee. I never had coffees like this during my childhood in India; they were usually made with an instant powder, topped with generous quantities of milk and sugar. I remember the taste of the buffalo milk, so creamy that a skin would form on the top of the drink if it was left a second too long.

I was only allowed to drink coffee on special occasions, which is why I can recall the taste. The explanation my grandmother gave was that drinking too much tea or coffee would make my skin darker, which was considered undesirable by everyone in the grown-up world. I would fight with her to let me have more of the creamy coffee, not caring about her warnings. The truth was probably that my grandmother wanted to avoid dealing with a caffeinated child. I wonder why she couldn't tell me the truth....

Perhaps my grandmother didn't know about the chemistry of caffeine or didn't think I would understand. She was a relatively educated woman for her time, but she knew very little about science and had only learned a few English words. She was married at the age of fifteen and became a mother by seventeen, so her priorities were her family and household rather than education and career. Despite her superstitions and old-fashioned ways, my grandmother was very maternal and caring. I had loved her company.

The cultural and generational gap between my grandmother's world and mine has now become so wide that if she were here now we would barely be able to talk to one another. But then, if she were here everything would have turned out to be completely different. I would be speaking fluent Hindi and we could have talked and laughed together – she always had a wicked sense of humour. She could sit with her snow-white hair in a bun, an areca nut in her mouth and tell funny stories for hours on end.

My favourite was the one in which she met my grandfather for the first-time: she had first disapproved of his village background and thought herself much superior for having been raised in a town, though she admitted that he was a strikingly handsome boy; in time she grew more attached to her husband than to anyone else, including her parents and seven brothers and sisters. Although I'd never met my grandfather, my grandmother's stories made him real to me. I knew how much she missed him because his framed photo was the first thing she looked at in the mornings.

My grandmother married into a well-off family in the small town of Dharna. My grandparents were landowners who had various rural properties and my grandfather had qualified as a lawyer. They were able to give their children the opportunity to study well and my father and uncle both chose to study Law like their father. My aunt also had the choice to work, but she wanted the family life instead. My mother was the only woman in the family who chose a career. She met my father at a Law college in Dharna. Theirs was an unusual kind of Hindu marriage for their time, as they had chosen each other instead of an arrangement being made between their parents. There were some disputes, I am told, but both families were educated and middle-class, so the match was eventually agreed upon. Vijay Uncle once told me that my mother was incredibly hard-working and had balanced both her work and family-life very well.

I have a few vague memories of my parents, but nothing very distinctive. I don't even feel their loss; you can't lose something you hardly remember having. What I do feel, though, is vagueness about myself, like a blurred photograph seen in half light. I would like at least a field of reference, to be able to trace my characteristics back to the two unknown individuals who created me.

* * *

Sitting here in the café, I have started writing down some of my unsequenced thoughts and memories in a pocket-sized notebook that I can carry around with me. So far, my musings appear unclear and confusing and I haven't come to any concrete conclusions about myself or my native land.

I used to love writing analytically but personal writing is another thing entirely. The things I wrote in my university essays came so easily in comparison to this, when I was not the subject of my own thoughts. I should enjoy the self-indulgence of this journey, the way many of my classmates did when they took gap years to 'see the world' or 'experience a new reality'.

A colleague at the bookstore told me once that her gap year travelling around South East Asia helped her realise what it meant to be English – it made her see, in relative terms, the culture she came from as opposed to the culture she did not come from. She gained a newfound appreciation for Sunday roasts, snowy Decembers, dry wit and the love of football, which were all things she associated with her family in Brighton.

After a while, I return to my aunt's house and spend some time in her garden. As I am walking in the courtyard, I am suddenly swept away by the fragrances wafting on the warm breeze: the smell of the moist, watered earth, the *Beli* and *Raat ki Raani* flowers mingling with the scent of the rustling *Neem* tree. Such fragrances evoke a memory of my childhood home, a longing to have it back and a hope that I am near enough at least to smell it.

But in another moment, I can smell an overpowering stench. I look out of the gate and see three small children carrying cow dung, probably to be made into cakes for burning as cooking fuel. I find this image unsettling, never having seen anything like it in London. The enchantment I felt is suddenly replaced by disappointment in the way things are here. Having ventured out into the streets of Delhi, I'm beginning to feel a strange anger and displacement in the lack of human concern I see all around me.

I don't remember feeling so uncomfortable in my native country when I was a child. I remember feeling like a fish swimming in the natural water of my home. I remember fearlessly running with bare feet in my grandmother's dusty courtyard, without a thought to the large ants or lizards that could have been hiding there. I remember embracing the heat when there was no electricity, using it as an opportunity to hunt for fireflies.

Now I shudder at the thought of a malaria-carrying mosquito and the dust on my feet itches inconveniently. I don't want to soak in sweat if the electricity goes out and I have come armed with a mini hand-fan just in case that happens. It annoys me that slums can exist alongside palace-like malls and that children can labour in the streets without anyone caring.

On one hand, I am revelling in the nostalgia of being here, but at the same time some of the sights and sounds are beginning to disturb and repulse me. I am judging this place through foreign eyes and I don't want to behave like an outsider in my motherland.

* * *

Over the next few days, I visit the most famous sights in Delhi: the Qutub Minar, India Gate, the Lotus Temple and Humayun's Tomb. In the evenings, I go into bookshops and flip through some classics. *Wuthering Heights, Things Fall Apart, Jane Eyre.* I also start reading some of the Indian writers who have become internationally renowned in order to see what they have to say about modern India. After a couple of days, the bookshop owner has begun to recognise me. One evening, he comments on the books I am buying by saying, "India is four things only: historical and modern, poor and prosperous. All these things are existing in a mix here!"

I am beginning to see the paradoxes myself and wonder if my roots lie somewhere in this mix or if it's become too late for me to find out anything authentic about my background here. I hope to God, if God exists, that I will find some memories of my parents preserved here, that I will be able to talk with conviction and belonging about the place that I came from.

No one here questions me about my background or my right to be here; it's an inner unease I have that makes me feel separate and doubtful about my mission. Even in London, it was more my own unease rather than the occasional stares that made me feel uncomfortable. I can live without a homeland, but if people expect me to talk about my culture and roots, then there are some things I need to feel certain about.

I have to stop now, stop trying to justify or analyse if coming here was a good idea. I'm here and there's no way to turn back. I have to hold onto the hope

I felt in Regent's Park. After all, I haven't even reached Dharna yet.

* * *

Archana Auntie reads the newspapers every morning with a steaming cup of *chai* poised in her left hand. She makes quiet tutting sounds and sometimes small comments expressing disapproval. I have noticed that her views are very rigid. She makes judgements against minority groups, suggesting that they should 'go home' to where they belong.

She makes me feel uneasy. Her words echo the racist statements made by some political groups against minority ethnics in Britain. I would like to challenge her. Where does anyone belong? God didn't divide the earth, I argue silently, thinking about Maria's view of the God that I'm not sure of myself.

I think of the Muslims in India, who are far more Indian than I am. Then my mind switches to the London bombings in July 2005. Those bombers were more British than I am: they were born and brought up in England. Yet, they associated themselves more with the fate of Islamic nations than with Britain. For them, culture and identity were ideas related to religion rather than nationality.

The kind of roots I'm searching for are neither nationalistic nor religious. I'm not quite sure what other kind of roots there are, maybe ancestral, cultural, or a combination of these things. I realise this sounds unclear. It seems you can't avoid associating a person with a nationality or religion when you think about their cultural background and ancestry. And then, ancestry is such a biological concept that I can't even say that it's really the right word. I am not looking to trace my family tree, only to understand the place my parents came from, the place where I was born, its customs, dialects, rhythms and traditions. What is it that defines someone's 'home'? Surely it's the character of the place they were born in? But that place then gets linked to a bigger idea: the idea of a country. I'm looking for a personal understanding of my homeland rather than a political one, but will I be able to separate the two things?

I remember a Muslim girl at university telling me that nationalism is considered undesirable in the *Qur'an*, because it undermines the brotherhood of souls by creating territorial division. Partition was one of those man-made divisions that tore millions of Hindus and Muslims from their homes.

It's unbelievable to think that the decisions made by men sitting in rooms can affect uncountable lives for generations to come. I don't know everything about the historical decisions that shaped this massive country I'm in, but I feel that the desire to separate and segregate people must stem from some insecure need – the need to preserve one collective identity by suppressing everything that is different from it.

It's the same dangerous game of oppositions that Maria told me about and that the postcolonial writers whose books I've been reading seem so aware of. It's been going on for years and is still happening today: America and Iraq, Israel and Palestine, Nazis and Jews, blacks and whites, capitalists and communists, imperialists and colonies, aristocrats and labourers, natives and immigrants.

In Britain I've seen how foreigners have been gradually integrated into a society which eventually realised its dependency on immigrant labour, especially in fields like healthcare. But I know there have been many tensions and problems in this process, which still exist in some pockets of British society. On the other hand, in places like America, Canada, South Africa and Australia, the outsiders have wielded the power all along and the indigenous people have been marginalised by the colonisers who entered their homelands. I know people in the UK who still feel proud of the British Empire without realising how oppressive it was.

I'm glad that India managed to free itself from that imperial oppression and that Britain has become a more tolerant country these days, but I am beginning to notice a different kind of oppressiveness in India right now. Here, I've noticed that there is almost no regulation of wealth and poverty, danger and safety, injustice and equality.

On top of the everyday chaos I can see all around, it looks as though prejudices of caste and skin colour have a direct impact on people's living conditions. To deal with this, the government seems to be enforcing irrational laws which it helplessly hopes will correct the country's deeply ingrained imbalances: the current affairs magazines here inform me that knowing the sex of the foetus is prohibited, that special college seats are allocated for specific castes, that women are exempt from wearing a motorbike helmet, amongst other rulings which can't possibly solve the real issues, even when they are followed. Then there are the daily reports of corruption and bribery which makes all the government's vain attempts at progress seem like empty gestures.

Reading the magazines and newspapers here, it terrifies me that various groups are trying to annihilate each other in order to enforce their power and identity. I know that this is something that's going on all over the world right now, but it is happening in a much more obvious way here because there are not enough controls in place to keep things from escalating.

Amidst the Indian media's continuous reports of power struggles, I have occasionally come across pictures of the Dalai Lama, who has created a Tibetan settlement in North India for refugees that have fled from their country. I am told that the Buddhist leader has decided on a non-violent protest against the occupation and violation of his homeland because his beliefs go against the use of violence. The Dalai Lama's stance is compared to Mahatma Gandhi's philosophy, another leader whose political decisions were greatly influenced by his religious beliefs. This thing called religion obviously has a powerful force: some kill for it whilst others become pacifists because of it. I ask myself how something as flimsy as religion can influence people to act with such determination. How can something invisible move some people to such a degree?

I am a Hindu, but to me that's just a label – a name that denotes something about my background rather than any philosophy that I believe in. Although I have seen strange things that suggest there are spirits all around us, I have no evidence to believe that there is anything more than that, and I certainly have no evidence of there being a personal God.

Some foolish, romantic part of me would like to think that human love has the capacity to see through differences. Adam and I never discussed the issue of our cultural differences, although it stared us in the face every day. Adam didn't believe in God or in destiny, only in what we create for ourselves. He believed in the power of human will over circumstances. That's why it frustrated him even more when I couldn't tell him anything about my ideas and feelings: he thought I had chosen to leave him out willingly.

Being with Adam would have fulfilled my ideal of destroying cultural barriers by uniting our different backgrounds: being with someone who is different from me yet who belongs with me. I didn't try hard enough to show him that I cared. Maybe he was right to say that I was afraid of happiness. Happiness can change into sorrow in the same way that life must eventually give way to death.

❑❑❑

Chapter 8

I watch the maid as she cooks silently in my aunt's kitchen. She pours water onto the rice and lights the stove. She grinds fresh spices on a stone slab with a chunk of varnished black brick. She grinds turmeric, ginger and cardamom. The turmeric glows with yellow moisture as it is crushed into a paste with water. No onion or garlic is cooked on a Tuesday because it is an auspicious day when my aunt fasts until sunset. This is not a strict fast and she allows herself to have fruit, milk, juices and tea. This is a vegetarian kitchen where egg is cooked occasionally but never fish, chicken or other kinds of meat. My aunt has given up meat and fish in her widowhood – it was not compulsory for her to do this, but it is a custom followed by most women on her husband's side of the family. She tells me she misses the taste of curried fish with rice, a favourite that she used to enjoy with her husband.

The rice steams on the gas hob and the maid drains the water from the kidney beans. Her name is Seema and she doesn't seem to notice me standing in the kitchen, fingering the spice jars absently as she works on with purpose. My aunt tells me that Seema is a trustworthy girl, the main provider for her family. She has two children and an alcoholic husband who beats her and her two boys when he gets too drunk, which he does quite often.

Unlike many uneducated people who go on reproducing children without the means to support them, Seema found out about her options and had an operation to stop herself conceiving again, mainly because she has enough trouble protecting the children she already has. My aunt tells me that Seema even contemplated leaving her husband, but her own mother pressurised her to stay with him and endure the violence. All this I hear from my aunt, but Seema barely says a word to me. She simply works quietly and leaves.

* * *

One afternoon, I walk out from the flat into the courtyard and then down the street to a nearby park. The wind is rustling soothingly and children are kicking a muddy ball on the patch of grass. I take a seat and breathe in the cool wintry air. I can feel something grazing my back. Tucked between the metal plates of the park bench is a small piece of yellowed paper. I pull it out and unfold the creases. There are small scribbles made in red pen along the margins: a paisley, a star, an eye. Underneath the scribbles, there are two verses:

They say go to Buddha
Or go to Mohammed
They say go to Jesus
Or go to Shiva -
I do not know where to go
So I choose to come instead straight to you
All truths spoken from human mouths
Divine truths are turned to dust in the world
You are the Gentle Love of my Heart
In your presence, all else disappears

There is no one around whom the poem could belong to, so I put it into my pocket. I don't believe in superstitions or signs, but it strikes me that these verses are a response to my recent thoughts about India and its divisions. The poem seems to be saying that religious doctrines don't really matter and that God exists beyond all boundaries and divisions. There have been a few rare moments in my life when I have looked at Nature and felt awed by the unexplainable mystery of life; this poem reminds me of that wonder.

On my way back to my aunt's house, I think about the idea of God expressed in the verses. I feel curious about the conviction of the mysterious poem, a conviction that extends beyond a mere certainty of physical life, into a deep knowing of what exists beyond. The poem asserts that it's not necessary to follow a path created by someone else, that the truth will reveal itself to the poet just as willingly as it revealed itself to Jesus, Mohammed or the Buddha. It says that it's not necessary to be anyone special, to be a leader, in order to find divine truth and spiritual love.

I have been struggling so much to accept simple, everyday reality that I can't imagine having a connection with anything metaphysical or spiritual. I have enough trouble living with the most basic thing about myself, which is my name. During most of my life in the UK, I have been enunciating and re-enunciating it to make people understand it – I have spelt and respelt it, explained its meaning to curious strangers over and over again. "L-A-X-M-I," I have to say loudly and clearly, "Yes, it does have a meaning: it means prosperity and it comes from the Hindu goddess of wealth." Even then, it is mispronounced and misspelt repeatedly. It's not anyone's fault, it's just an inconvenience I have learned to live with. Some British Indians I know anglicise their names to make things easier, and some are cautious enough to give their children international sounding names, like Natasha, Saara, Neel or Arun.

Here in India, nobody asks me about my name. They don't think twice about it when they hear it. The waiter in the café notes it down swiftly whenever I order anything; he pronounces it with precision when the coffee is ready for me. I have even seen variations of my name on shop windows and billboards: *Mahalaxmi Stationers, Laxmi Salwaar Suits, Dhanlaxmi Chemists.* This is not really as much of a comfort as I thought it would be. Granted, it makes things easier to have my name so easily understood. But at the same time I find it irritating that the name which made me painfully different and was even thought 'exotic' at times has now become completely unremarkable.

* * *

I pack for tomorrow. My bus leaves Delhi at eight pm and will arrive in Dharna at seven the next morning. It's an eleven-hour journey.

I re-organise my clothes and toiletries, which have been largely untouched during these few days in Delhi. Living out of a suitcase for this time has shown me how very little I actually need for self-preservation: food, water, soap and a few clothes. That's all anyone needs, however more we may desire to have. I thought I would miss things like hair dryers, cosmetics and accessories, but I'm actually glad to be free of all that clutter.

A pale green lizard skims across the wall above me before halting, motionless against the mahogany wardrobe.

It licks its translucent lips with a quick flicker. The afternoon heat cajoles all kinds of insects into the house and the small ants, spiders, cockroaches are swiftly hunted and eaten by these house lizards. On this level, the food chain operates instinctively and effectively, unlike the choices we humans make about our food. This makes me think back to what it was that prompted my decision to become a vegetarian when I was ten.

I would like to think it was a moral decision, taking account of the unnecessary bloodshed and ecological waste involved in eating meat, but I know it was really the taste of the minced meat and fatty chicken we were served in boarding school that made my stomach turn with disgust. I used to love the fish and mutton my grandmother cooked in Dharna, lean cut and spiced up in rich gravy with cloves and ginger. But even if that were served to me now, I could never go back to eating meat. Something has changed for good and cannot be undone.

* * *

I dream of my grandmother, singing holy verses in her stone-floored prayer room, standing with bare feet before the idols of Ganesh, Krishna, Shiva, Parvati, Hanuman and many others. She finishes her morning *puja*, covers her hair with the end of her white sari and steps into the adjoining kitchen. The fragrance of incense fills the house. I run into the kitchen and watch as she pops an areca nut into her mouth. She turns on the gas stove to boil the milk and makes *ghee* from the cream. She allows me to dip my finger into the cup of cream and have a taste. I stand on tiptoe next to her, peering up to see what she is doing. Her cotton sari feels smooth and comforting near my arms.

Then the dream changes into my recurring nightmare. I am on the moon, with the old whiskered man standing in front of me. He asks his usual question, and says he will give me a treat if I answer correctly. "Who are you?" he asks me with a jaunty wink. I open my mouth, not knowing what will come out, but before I can say anything, I realise my mouth is gagged. I struggle to speak for a few moments but nothing happens. A while later, I'm awake.

I turn onto my side and think of Adam. The memory of his open smile fills me with longing. I remember the warmth of his hands around mine and the fragrance of his cologne mixed with his delicate human scent. Intimacy came easily when it was about physical expression, but when it came to words, we began to falter. Even when he looked into my eyes, I would turn away from his gaze, as though I didn't want him to see too much. Or perhaps it was a fear of showing too little: a fear that there was nothing within.

I go into the bathroom to wash my eyes. A swallow comes back to its nest in the metal grill outside the window. Two of its eggs have just hatched, and it is feeding its young constantly throughout the day. There is a pool of light falling from the street lamp into the room and I can see the clothes I've laid out for tomorrow's journey: a pair of loose brown trousers, a short cotton *kurta*, brown leather sandals. Everything else is packed away.

I gaze around the bedroom and receive a shock when I see a figure hiding in the corner. I flick on the light switch out of fear, only to find that it is my own reflection in the long mirror on the other side of the room: an oval face with what people have said are becoming features. I see myself as an observer, with no sense of identification that the image is a reflection of myself. It is just the form of a girl who could be anyone. I turn out the light and fall back onto the pillow.

❑❑❑

Chapter 9

The next morning I bathe with water from the bucket instead of using the shower because the water has not come to the neighbourhood today and this method ensures that I use only what is needed. I can hear people in the building next door complaining about the water shortages.

I pour two jugs full of water over my head before shampooing my hair and soaping my skin. I scrub and wash out the lather with water and it gives me a cooling thrill as it splashes onto my warm skin. Drying myself off quickly, I pull on my trousers and *kurta*. Sitting on the bed, I unfold my compact to look closely into the mirror.

I need barely a drop of moisturiser because the heat in the afternoons makes my skin moist with perspiration. Already I can feel a light sweat breaking out over my body, even though my aunt insists it's getting cold in Delhi now. I take out a bottle of deodorant and spray a generous coating all over myself. The smell of magnolia floods the room, bringing back a fragrance from my life in London. I have only been away a few days, but it already feels like months have passed.

I am packed and ready for the bus ride to Dharna. My aunt gives me her blessings for a safe trip and asks me to call her every weekend. I nod as I open the car door. I stop at a bank on the way to withdraw some cash and, while standing in the queue, I notice that everyone around me is speaking English, even young children. From the car window, the driver can hear them too and he complains to himself that no one speaks proper Hindi anymore.

"That's the Delhi fashion for you," he tells me disapprovingly in clear Hindi. "They only use Hindi if it is to insult someone. They think Hindi is inferior."

"Oh, right," I mumble, wondering if this is just a tendency that has developed in the rapidly westernising metropolis of Delhi or if I'll encounter the same thing in Dharna.

As I reach the bus depot, I feel a surge of nervous nausea. The depot is crammed and dirty; it is teeming with disorder and I don't want to enter there alone. But I have to do it – it's too late to turn back. After roaming across the bus stops, I finally find my waiting area where two other people are standing. I put my rucksack down and pull my bottled water out from the front pocket. It tastes dissatisfyingly lukewarm.

A begging child in rags taps my knee and assertively announces the word, 'money'. I say I'm sorry and shake my head and he moves on. My heart is still thumping in my chest and my knees are shaking. Although the sun is out and the temperature is pleasantly warm, I am beginning to feel cold from panic. Will I be able to manage alone? Is it safe to travel and live on my own in this crazy country? I take a few deep breaths to calm myself. I haven't come all this way to be put off now.

After a long wait, a worn old bus marked 'Dharna' pulls up in front of me. I pass my rucksack to a boy who numbers it with chalk and pushes it into a side storage compartment underneath the vehicle. I climb the bus and find seat number eight, the number scrawled onto my ticket. The bus is largely empty, so I have two seats to myself. I recline in my chair and look outside. The purple-tinted windows make it difficult to see anything more than the tops of people's heads under the glowing sky.

The bus lurches forward and I try to sleep. In my half consciousness, I watch the landscapes change. Urban traffic, noise and dust turn into mustard fields and later into forests. I slip in and out of dreams where I am metamorphosed into other people: a mixed-race woman arguing with her white father and African mother, a monk in Spain wearing a long brown garb and sandals while walking peacefully on a green hill, a man riding a horse long a riverside. I also dream of snakes shedding their skins and entering into a murky lake. These dreams disturb me but I am glad I did not see the whiskered old man in any of them.

Hours pass, the sky darkens and then eventually some light begins to reach through the coloured glass once again. I wipe my eyes with a dampened tissue and look out at the lush green valleys growing tea leaves and some plants that have curly vegetables sprouting in watery soil. The bus curves across the Himalayan mountains.

The other passengers begin to stir and talk. A while later, the driver stops for refreshments at a Punjabi *dhaba* next to a waterfall. I sit outdoors in the cool mountain air and order a *masala chai* with vegetable *pakoras*. There is a small terrace looking out towards the waterfall, where foaming water rushes down the mountainside, reddened by the colour of the earth. I sip the sugary spiced tea and bite into a hot cauliflower coated in gram-flour batter. The mixture of salt and sugar fills my mouth with flavour and rouses me from a sleepy daze. There are families sitting all around me, enjoying their breakfasts and chatting with excitement about the relatives they are going to visit or the temples they are going to see.

When we climb back onto the bus, the driver puts on a Hindi music cassette. I listen contentedly to the upbeat tunes expressing romantic love and longing and for a moment my mind is totally empty of thoughts.

We move down from the heights towards Dharna, which is situated at a low altitude in the mountainous state of Himachal Pradesh. After another hour has passed the bus draws into a tiny depot and the conductor announces that we have arrived.

* * *

Strangely enough, I suddenly recognise the streets and some of the houses here. It is a miniscule town where one can walk from one end to the other in forty minutes. The roads are mainly like dust paths but they are dappled with greenery and every now and again there is a bright cherry tree hanging out from somebody's garden.

I look at my map and manage to locate the road where Mr Chakram lives, the man who will be my landlord for the coming months. Shanti is the name of the road and it is just adjacent to the road where I think my grandmother's house used to be. A lump forms in my throat as I contemplate visiting that house again. My initial panic has subsided and given way to curiosity. I wonder who lives in that house now.

I ring Mr Chakram's doorbell and a small old man in a neatly pressed shirt and trousers answers the bell. As soon as I introduce myself, his small eyes light up with surprise and warmth. Mr Chakram leads me into the drawing room and calls a young boy to make tea for us.

Mr Chakram tells me that Tulip Marg is the name of the street where my grandmother's house used to be and this is the road he takes me to after we have finished the last dregs of the spicy tea. I see that there are no tulips on the Tulip Marg, but there are rose bushes and mango trees.

"I thought you would like to stay in your grandmother's house," Mr Chakram tells me as we walk down the street. He pulls out a key from his breast pocket. "I bought the place from your uncle after her death and it has been empty for some time. I just had it cleaned yesterday and it's still in good condition."

I am a little taken aback at hearing that I'll be living in the same place I did when I was a child. The door creaks open and reveals a red speckled stone floor. A wave of nostalgia engulfs me. There are a few old armchairs and a dining table in the first room. We walk through the adjoining room, which has a bed and two more doorways, one leading to the back garden and one to the bathroom. I regretfully notice the Indian-style toilet which I will have to get used to. All the main rooms of the house are on the ground floor and there is a narrow stairwell at the side which leads up the storeys of the adjoining building onto a flat, open roof where I remember flying kites with other children from the neighbourhood: buoyantly coloured, red, orange and green kites that glided up and filled the amber evening skies.

Mr Chakram leads me back through the main living space and into the kitchen which links to it on the other side. It is dark, cold and empty, but the structure is exactly the same as I remember. I instinctively walk round the corner where I know there is a prayer room. In disbelief I see that all the statues of the gods are lined there exactly as they were twenty years ago. My grandmother's hands may well have been the last human hands to touch these statues. There is a haunting atmosphere in this room, where the memory of faith and devotion rests alongside the memory of death.

I was in this house when she died. I was the one who found her. I thought she was sleeping. I shook her and tried to wake her and when she didn't wake I ran next door to get help from whoever was there at the time. Archana Auntie came the next day and took me away with her after the funeral rites were performed. That was the last time I was in Dharna.

❏❏❏

Chapter 10

After Mr Chakram has left, I place my rucksack against the low bed and lie down on the hard mattress. The fan whirrs gently in the background, but there is not much need for it at this time of year, especially now that the sun has gone down. It is dinner time and my stomach is rumbling with hunger, but there is no food in the house. I decide to go out and see if any of the local shops are still open.

I lock the front door with the heavy brass lock Mr Chakram has given me and turn towards the narrow road leading towards the marketplace. Every now and then, a car tries to squeeze past riskily. The cyclists and other pedestrians walk on fearlessly when cars honk behind them in the semi-darkness, but I cannot help but stop cautiously in order to let the cars pass. The traffic is reckless and I am not used to dodging the vehicles when they come too close.

Ten minutes later I reach a row of shops. My sandals and the bared parts of my feet have been covered by a powdering of dust which is caked between my toes. It occurs to me that being back in India has brought me face to face with hundreds of diseases which I am not immune to. I should have been more careful and taken the recommended travel vaccines before coming back here after so long.

There is risk everywhere: in the water, the food, the air and the surroundings. There is the risk of tetanus, polio, typhoid and even rabies from the countless stray dogs roaming the streets. I try to remember what Vijay Uncle told me: *only eat piping hot food, only drink bottled water, use mosquito nets and insect repellent every day.* I will have to be more aware.

Last week in Delhi I nearly drank water straight from the tap the way I am accustomed to doing in London. Just that one mistake could have critical consequences. I can't help but stare in awe at the two bare-footed children running in the filth in front of me without a fear in the world.

I scan the row of shops. They are similar to British corner shops, crammed full of knick-knacks, snacks, household goods and stationery. I could get some bread and snacks for dinner, maybe buy a few vegetables to cook, or I could try the little restaurant next to the shops, which is royally named *Swad Mahal*, meaning 'the palace of flavour'. My growling hunger leads me into the restaurant, hoping that it really does offer some flavoursome food, because it definitely does not live up to the claim of being a palace.

The restaurant is very worn out and shabby-looking but it appears to be reasonably clean. The surfaces have clearly been wiped recently and the tables are neatly arranged. An eager waiter in a white pressed shirt hurries towards me with a menu in his hand. There is just one other family in the restaurant and plenty of empty tables. I gather that it's still quite early for dinner in India, where most people seem to eat after eight the way Archana Auntie does.

I pray to the God who may or may not exist that the food here is hygienic and will not give me dysentery or cholera. I shouldn't have paid so much attention to Bhavna Auntie's medical books when I was younger because it seems that at this very moment I have a vast knowledge of diseases. I put the threatening bacterial thoughts out of my mind as I look through the menu.

My mouth is soon watering as I read the misspelt descriptions of the starters, curries and sundries. There is *Paneer Lajabab*, which is described as an Indian 'cheez' cooked in a special gravy made with tomatoes and cream. There is also *Begun Bharta*, sizzling aubergine roasted with spices. I have never seen so much vegetarian food on a menu list. I choose the *paneer* with two plain *rotis*.

Waiting for the food to appear, I suddenly feel very awkward sitting alone in a restaurant. Although I am wearing an Indian *kurta*, the family sitting in the corner of the restaurant keep glancing at me as though I'm wearing the emperor's new clothes. I wonder what it is about me that seems strange to them. Then I realise that it's probably the fact that I'm alone.

It is around eight o'clock now and for a young female to be sitting by herself at a restaurant is unusual here. I suppose it's unusual in any culture and it does make me feel a little uncomfortable. But I have no choice here: I don't know anyone personally and there's no food in the house. I pull out a book from my cotton shoulder-bag so as to look preoccupied, but I can't seem to concentrate on *Travels On My Elephant* anymore.

The book is about India but I haven't been able to read a page of it since I got to India. I was fully absorbed by it when I was far from this place, when it was unreachable in physicality. Now that I'm here, I'm finding my experience of it to be so overwhelming that I can't identify with the experiences of the author, his mission being so different from my own.

The waiter brings my food in ornate little pots and true to its claim, the food is deliciously full of flavour. The *paneer* is delectably soft and almost melts on my tongue as I wrap it with *roti* and take satisfying mouthfuls. I ask the waiter for two bottles of water so I can take them back to the house afterwards. When I have finished, the waiter asks me in Hindi if I enjoyed the meal and I reply that it was delicious. He nods grimly as though my answer is a mere confirmation of what he already knows and graciously lets me out.

The sky is now pitch-black. There are just a few dim lights glowing from shops and houses but there are no street lamps. Thankfully, I have a torch for the walk back. I buy some milk and bread for the next morning from a small store in a side street before turning homeward.

❑❑❑

Chapter 11

A darkly-clad man with greying hair is sitting behind the desk. Outside this pristine little office, the rest of Dharna High School is preparing for a day of lessons. The man points to the empty chair across from himself and I quietly take a seat.

"You must be Laxmi," he says slowly and without enthusiasm, "Laxmi Gupta from the UK."

"Yes," I reply. "Thank you for this opportunity for me to teach here."

"Not at all," he says. "As you probably know, I am Mr Agarwal, the Headmaster of this school." He pauses and rubs his right temple frowningly.

"Now, Ms Gupta, I am sure you know your subject well enough, but there are some important school procedures I need to clarify to you." He looks at me sternly, like I've already committed an offence. I shrink down in my chair, feeling like a teenager once again, facing a hearing from the adult world.

"First of all," he continues, his voice rising in volume, "the relationship between pupils and teachers must be kept formal at all times. I know that in *the West* there is an informal and almost lax attitude towards discipline and this is also the reason why children in European schools have so little respect..."

He pauses again and looks at me pointedly. "I have taught Chemistry in England myself, Ms Gupta, so I know from personal experience how ill-behaved the pupils can be. Their attitude was appalling."

I can hear an undercurrent of bitterness in his carefully enunciated words. He glares at me and shakes his head. "We don't let students contest the authority of their teachers by calling them by their names or even surnames. It is always either Sir or Madam."

I nod to show my understanding of the rules.

"Also, we check that pupils are wearing the correct uniform and they are not allowed to leave the classroom during lessons, not even to use the washrooms. They must make sure they are properly prepared for each lesson and if they show signs of sloppy behaviour, it must be discussed with their parents..."

Mr Agarwal goes on. I think back to lessons with my unconventional Biology teacher, Mr Maxwell, who used to make learning fun and memorable for us by making jokes about bacteria or the digestive system of a cow. I'd like to be the kind of teacher the students enjoy spending time with. But it sounds like Mr Agarwal would prefer me to be a stern and morose pedagogue who makes her pupils learn by rote. I'll have to see what the other teachers in the school are like, whether or not they follow Mr Agarwal's example.

Finally, Mr Agarwal gets up and smiles for the first time. His features soften considerably. "Come with me now," he says firmly. "Let us introduce you to some of your colleagues."

I follow him down a chalky white corridor. Our feet clunk against the polished granite floors; there is muffled chatter, barely audible and the twittering of a hundred different birds from the gardens on the other side of the school.

"There is a lovely botanical garden next door, Ms Gupta, you may want to frequent it during your lunch break one day. It is very peaceful."

"Yes, that sounds nice."

"I often go in there myself."

"Oh right," I mumble in acknowledgement. I make a mental note to avoid the gardens during school hours, in case of accidental sightings by Mr Agarwal's critical eyes.

"Ah, here we are, this is the staffroom."

He turns the rusted brass handle of a green door and it opens with a whining groan. Several faces suddenly turn towards me, judging and staring at me with undisguised curiosity. Mr Agarwal begins introducing me and hands begin to extend themselves to shake mine. Everything becomes a blur as I move from greeting one bespectacled teacher to another: Jaya Mehta, the Maths teacher; Subhash Madan, the Hindi teacher; Neelam Biswas, the History teacher.... Not all of them are in fact bespectacled, but they all exude that teacherish air of bookish knowledge and self-importance.

It is hard to tell what they are really like, whether they are all conservative like Mr Agarwal or secretly liberal and fun-loving under their guise of seriousness. It's never been my preference to teach anyone anything and I am not technically qualified to teach, although I know a lot about English language and literature from my degree subject. But there's little else I can do here in Dharna. I don't know how well I will fit into this strange category of teachers.

My first task is to observe some lessons taught by an English teacher who will soon be leaving the school for a better-paid job. I decide to take this exercise seriously, since I have no official teacher training. The teacher I'm observing is Mathew De Souza, a tall and thin young man with a generous smile and a slightly effeminate aura which I find comforting.

I sit on a table at the side of the room as he addresses his Year Eleven class. He seems very relaxed and natural, gently explaining which texts are on the syllabus and what kind of work each of them will involve. This will be the second time this year that the group has encountered Shakespeare: they read *Romeo and Juliet* for their last exams and this year it will be *Othello*. The students look a little afraid, but I am quite sure that this year group can read at a relatively advanced level because they have chosen English as one of their core subjects for their final secondary school exams – I've heard the teachers referring to it as 'ten plus two', which seems to be the equivalent of A-levels or IB. The students speak very little, so I cannot pinpoint any individual attributes; they seem like a collective mass with a single, silent and timid personality shared between them.

After the class, Matthew tells me to remember that all of my students know English as their second language, even though it may seem like they are quite fluent because they have been learning the language for such a long time.

"This is even more so the case because they pick up a lot of English from watching TV. But you have to be wary of their grammatical understanding and try to make them follow the British usage as much as possible."

I laugh and point out that I myself once learned English as a second language, and even native speakers get their grammar wrong from time to time. Remembering my college lectures, I also mention that every kind of

English is supposed to be equally relevant as a testament of the way different cultures have adopted the English language to suit themselves.

"Maybe in theory," says Matthew, smiling with his eyelids closed. "In practice, the school wants them to learn the English of the English. It gives students a better chance in the corporate world, where people still think British English is the best. Obviously we can't stop them from speaking Indianised English, but we have to correct them as much as possible."

This is another of the school's old-fashioned ways that I'll have to get used to. As Mathew hands me some paperwork and explains how the classes are timetabled, I notice he has an easy manner and casual grace. We walk down the polished stone corridors up to the staffroom just as the bell rings three times. The noise in the staffroom is almost as loud as the students' chatter outside in the playground. Lunch boxes are clanking impatiently and a medley of aromas seduces my nostrils as my eyes feast upon a dozen different lunches. One teacher has a neatly wrapped *dosa* with pickle; another has egg-fried rice. I look down at my handbag where my cheese sandwich is hidden. I reach for it and prepare myself for its disappointingly predictable taste. The two small slices of Indian bread barely do enough to whet my appetite.

Just then I see the Hindi teacher, Subhash Madan, walking towards me purposefully. I look up as he thrusts his lunchbox in front of my eyes. The delectable smell of fresh chapattis and spiced aubergine enters my nostrils and leaves my mouth watering.

"Please have some," Subhash says. "Your lunch was looking very minimal."

I laugh, but quickly resume a serious demeanour in case he thinks I'm laughing at him. I take some of the food he offers, being careful not to touch it with the hand I have been eating with, as sharing germs is something many Indian families disapprove of. Subhash asks me a few questions about London which I answer politely, thanking him for sharing his food with me. He appears to be in his early thirties, with dark eyes and short hair greying slightly at his temples. He has a thin, trimmed moustache which actually complements his sharp features, something I think few men are able to pull off. In his crisply ironed rose-coloured shirt and black trousers, he exudes a school-boyish air which contrasts the lines of thought and wisdom that have begun to appear around his eyes.

As the bell begins to ring again, the teachers start packing up their lunches, washing their hands and tidying their books and papers for the afternoon's lessons. My next class comprises a Year Seven group which is all girls. As I step into the room, wide eyes stare at me with deep curiosity. They are beautifully innocent eyes, all lined with black *kajal*. People say the kohl protects against the 'evil eye' or ill intentions. Mathew introduces me to the class, and I write down all of their names so I can memorise them for the next day. After Matthew has left the class, I ask the class if they have any questions for me, their new teacher for the next academic year. A dozen hands rise into the air all at once.

"Where are you from?"

"Where were you born?"

"What are your hobbies?"

"Who is in your family?"

I answer each of their questions one by one. Before I know it, the class is over and I have not been able to ask a single question. Tomorrow, it's my turn to get answers. I already have some idea of their personalities. Chaitrali is the bright spark of the class, always using the best English she can and correcting other students' mistakes at every opportunity. Vani is the constant chatterbox. Saraswati is the excitable one who can't help letting out a squeal every now and then. Their sweet voices and innocent curiosity is very endearing.

As I walk back towards my grandmother's house at the end of the school day, I see Subhash Madan swinging onto his bicycle to make the journey home. He has a lean frame and looks very carefree gliding away towards the light. From the back I see that his hair is cut very short, close to the scalp. Perhaps he shaved his head for a religious occasion quite recently. I don't know him at all, but there is something I find very likeable about him. He comes across as a good person, which I think means someone who has consideration for others and compassion for the world, perhaps tries not to hurt others deliberately and thinks about the consequences of his actions. His family members are probably important to him and they'll probably be responsible for choosing a spouse for him, if he isn't already settled. I'm sure most of the teachers in the school have already had or are due to have an arranged marriage. Even Matthew, who is a Christian, discreetly mentioned that his parents are looking for a bride for him. If I had grown up in this town and if my parents were alive, then I'd probably be willing to accept an arranged marriage myself.

❏❏❏

Chapter 12

It is Saturday morning which means no school for most teachers, although the children still need to attend sports activities in the school grounds. I wake up early and see the yolk-like sun rising from beyond the hills. I have a lot to do today and the first thing on my list is a visit to the market. I need vegetables, bread, milk, detergent and some more cooking pots and pans. Mr Chakram has furnished the place with most things: an old fridge, a television, an ancient-looking microwave, even a washing machine which is basically a swirling bucket. Everything in the house speaks of the past; the furniture is second-hand and marked with memories

– taints, scratches, children's graffiti. I don't know whose stories these are, but they are not mine and I feel a bit like an intruder visiting upon other people's privacy.

The roads are remarkably deserted for a Saturday morning. I walk briskly into the town centre, practising the Hindi phrases I might need to use. As the vegetables come into view, I stop to check if they have everything I want. They have it all and more. There are no modern malls around here, but there is still plenty of variety.

"*Bolo*, Madam," one of the market vendors calls out to me. I ask him to give me some green peppers, potatoes and tomatoes. Next, I visit the fruit stalls and the corner shop. So far I have spent three-hundred rupees on my weekly shopping, which is around five pounds. It may not be much for a tourist, but it's more than the daily wage of most labourers in India.

As I turn back towards the house, I hear someone calling my name. "Miss Laxmi! Hello!" It's Subhash Madan, the Hindi teacher.

"Oh, hello Subhash – I mean, Mr Subhash. Please call me Laxmi."

"Errr, okay... Miss Laxmi, do you want to see Dharna? I can show you many sights. You are new here and living alone, so it may be useful."

I begin to hesitate but Subhash Madan is quite insistent.

"At least see the riverside," he says. "It is very beautiful."

I reluctantly agree, although I am a little confused by Subhash Madan's willingness to waste his morning with someone he barely knows. Does he not have anything better to do than take a stranger to the riverside? I guess he doesn't have the pressing family commitments I'd imagined he had.

"You know, Miss Laxmi – sorry, sorry, Laxmi – I always like to get acquainted with new people. It helps me to learn about different – how do you say it – different ways of seeing the world."

"Yes," I say. "You get to see different perspectives on life."

The glare of sun causes a stream of light to pass across Subhash Madan's face. He nods cheerfully. Again, I notice how attractive he is, with his broad smile and richly tanned skin. The sleeves of his shirt are folded up to his elbows, and he has a tightly rolled newspaper in his left hand.

"So, what is your background, Laxmi?" He asks as we reach the riverside. "You are obviously an Indian by birth."

The openness of his questions and the lack of judgement in his eyes make me feel comfortable and I decide to try and answer this difficult question. This is very strange for me, but for some reason, the anxiety I usually feel in sharing my past has momentarily dissolved.

"My family is actually from here," I reply in a matter-of-fact tone. Then everything begins to come out in a splurge of unstoppable sentences. "I was born here in Dharna and lived here for a part of my childhood. My parents were involved in a road accident when I was two, so then my paternal grandmother looked after me in her house on Tulip Marg. When she passed away I went to stay with my uncle in England. I was seven at that time. I went to a boarding school and then to college. I never visited India in between. I really can't remember much more about my childhood. It's all a bit of a blur."

"Oh, I'm very sorry to hear about your parents," Subhash says with a note of sympathy. Then he adds with surprise, "This is your first time in India since childhood?"

"Yes."

"I don't know how you managed to stay away for so long. I know I am partial, but I could not stay far from my motherland for so long."

I smile and do not answer. Subhash tells me how he used to play cricket here after school and I visualise his childhood in this place. I imagine laughter, jokes, his mother shouting at him for staying out late. He talks a lot. He tells me about the bridge which is haunted by the ghost of a woman who drowned herself here four hundred years ago, about the types of fish that swim in the river, about the Maharaja's family members who have now lost all their wealth. I begin to feel very comfortable in his company, and the hours pass unknowingly like the moving river. As it starts getting late, Subhash leaves me outside my house and waves goodnight.

I enter the house and lock the door behind me. All of a sudden, I feel incredibly alone and lost, like a candle just went out in a dark room. Could I possibly be missing a person who I don't even know? It seems ridiculous. Subhash Madan is a stranger. I must be far too desperate and lonely if I'm missing him.

Chapter 13

The following Monday, I come across a curious character. Her name is Nina Srivastava and she is the Chemistry teacher. She has just returned from an extended holiday in Kerala.

Nina Srivastava seems to have no inhibitions. I know personal space is not emphasised as much in Indian society as it is in the UK, but this particular teacher is forthright to the point of being interfering. The other teachers feel it too and they squirm uncomfortably while talking to her.

She asks prying questions without blinking an eyelid. She doesn't seem to realise when she is being rude. In the chatter of the narrow staffroom, Nina Srivastava's voice is the loudest anyone can hear. It is a girlishly shrill, penetrating voice, comically at odds with the large framed woman projecting it.

On her first day back at the school, Nina Srivastava spots me as an unfamiliar face in the staffroom and loudly asks no one in particular, "Who is this girl?" She must know that I can hear her.

Subhash answers her question in his friendly way, but I do not hear his explanation of who I am. Then she looks at me with astonishment, which makes me feel like I have done something inappropriate, like forgetting to wear any clothes. I look down at myself to make sure there is nothing odd about me. The next thing I know, the stern-looking woman is marching towards me with an air of purpose. She stretches out her arm defiantly.

"Hello, my name is Nina Srivastava. You look like a very interesting person."

"Hello," I reply, a little confused by her analysis of my character. "I'm Laxmi. I don't think there is anything particularly interesting about me."

"Oh, but there is," Nina declares. "You are not a local person. There is something... different about you. I have an eye for such things."

I can't help laughing at her statement. I am wearing a traditional Indian tunic, my skin is brown, my hair dark, just like everyone else's. Without having spoken to me, how could she have known about my being 'different'?

Just then, Subhash approaches the conversation. "Nina, I have only just told you she is from the UK, so now you think she is a foreigner. I don't think Laxmi is any different from the rest of us," He says with a smile. "I suppose if you observe her language and accent, there are small differences."

"Yes," Nina says emphatically, "but it is also something in her behaviour, I think." Then, without another word, she looks at her watch and swiftly leaves the room.

"Actually, she is a strange person here," Subhash laughs. I decide not to say anything against Nina, but I am grateful to Subhash for defending me and for not thinking of me as a foreigner. Ever since I have started teaching at the school, Subhash has shown a protective kindness towards me. Technically, I am a foreigner, without Indian nationality, citizenship and the right to vote.

We begin talking about the school's history and I fall back into the same sense of ease I felt when I was with Subhash at the riverside. I no longer notice the difference of his English or the staccato of his pronunciation. He has begun to understand me more easily too, no longer asking me to repeat myself as much. He tells me about the secular style of the school building, which has attributes of both Hindu and Muslim architecture: eastern *swastika* shapes etched evenly into the curved pillars that line the roofed walkways.

The focus of the building is its burnt, browned playing field. There are classrooms facing the field from all four sides, with concrete paths connecting each of the six large buildings. The largest of these is the administrative building, where visitors are first greeted, through which the children walk every morning, and adjacent to which lies the large auditorium for special events and assemblies. Every morning, the children have to stand outside, so that they can practise marching exercises in the morning sun.

"It's a bit exhausting for them, isn't it?" I say to Subhash. "They have to do a whole exercise routine before their school day and have PE lessons on top of that."

"It builds their stamina," Subhash explains simply. I realise that these children are not accustomed to a lazy lifestyle of burgers, pizzas and play-stations like the elite crowds in the malls of New Delhi. They are middle-class Indians whose parents are reasonably well-educated; their fathers are mostly bankers, teachers, officials, and their mothers are generally homemakers. They are not aware of western habits like watching MTV on Sunday mornings or heating up a frozen snack in the microwave. In their relative experience, marching exercises are acceptable, as are traditional Indian meals, *pujas*, helping with the housework and studying on weekends.

"Come," Subhash gestures towards the door, "I will show you my favourite place in this school. We still have ten minutes before the next lesson starts."

We walk to the opposite side of the building. Behind the whitewashed walls, there are several Banyan trees, their arms planted into the soil as if they are searching for a treasure deep within the earth. The shaded grass below the trees is thick and green, unlike the lawn in the centre of the school, upon which the sun shines directly, day after day.

Subhash opens a creaky old wooden door and we enter a world of silence. The school library is large and spacious; the air inside is musty with the smell of ancient books. A lone librarian sits behind the main desk, reading a copy of *India Today*. He has a goatee beard and small eyes, with a long angular noise that lends him an odd dignity. He looks like he is in some sort of a uniform, wearing brown sandals, navy trousers and a pressed white shirt. Subhash tells me in a whisper that his name is Mahesh Kumar. Hearing the mention of his name, the librarian looks up at us and nods.

I am enchanted by the school's impressive collection of books, carefully preserved in hard bound covers and plastic jackets. Some of the books are very old; many are first editions. I run my finger across the spine of *Wuthering Heights*, bound in a royal blue, gold-embossed hardback cover. There is not a speck of dust on it.

As if reading my mind, Subhash whispers, "Mahesh maintains this library very well. He has a great respect for books, which is lucky for language teachers like us. We can borrow up to ten books for one month at a time."

"Wow, I'll probably spend hours in here," I confess.

Subhash looks pleased and says, "Nothing wrong with that. I already spend hours in this place."

Once we step outside, Subhash asks me an unexpected question. "So why did you return here after so long, Laxmi?" he asks.

I look into his gentle face and find myself trying to explain my complex decision to come back to Dharna.

"It's hard for me to explain," I begin. "London is now my home, the place I'm used to, the place where I'll live my life. But there's always been something missing there because my cultural roots, my parents' history, it's all buried somewhere else. I wanted to come here to find out about my birthplace, to get some sense of cultural identity."

After Maria, Subhash has been the only person I've shared my inner thoughts with to this extent. I don't understand why I've allowed him to know so much about me in such a short space of time. Perhaps it's because I know I'll be leaving this place, so there's nothing to lose by revealing my insecurities to him. But I think it's more than that: Dharna has opened a door for me.

The political injustices I felt in Delhi have seeped away here in Dharna's quiet setting, where the frustrations of being in a developing country are less obvious. I feel I can play a different role in this place and my reservations have loosened because I don't feel the need to justify who I am here. I especially don't feel the need to justify myself to Subhash, who seems to accept my words without judgement and obviously believes I have a right to be in India.

"But do you think understanding the ways of India will help you feel more sure of yourself?" Subhash asks after a while.

"I really don't know," I reply.

I am teaching *White Fang* to my Year Seven students, half of whom are keenly making notes of every word I say, whilst the other half gaze here and there, their minds quickly losing grasp of the information I am giving them. One girl is playing with her hair band and I am quite sure she has not taken in a single word I have said about the novel's language. I try to remember some tips from my reference book, *Learning to Teach*, which I brought back from London. I decide to change the lesson format so that it incorporates some of the tips the book recommended for keeping children's attention. This means abandoning the format of the school's *Manual for English Lessons*, which the Headmaster has asked me to follow.

I ask the girls to sit in groups and write a play version of what has happened in the book so far – they have already read the first half of the story during the previous year and I want to make sure they remember the plot so far before we move on.

At first the class is confused, but one of the brighter girls in the class quickly takes the initiative to form her group and begins writing, telling each team member which character they will play. Some of the other girls watch her and begin doing the same. A hum of voices soon fills the room, and time begins to speed by. I can tell by the end of the session that the girls have enjoyed the class. Looking at the excited smiles on their faces as they leave the classroom, I feel, after a long time, as if I have done something worthwhile with my time.

❑❑❑

Chapter 14

Four months have passed like a rapid stream. My classes are going smoothly and the students are progressing well. Subhash and I have lunch together every day now – every school day, that is. We usually sit alone outside the library, where there is a cobbled stone bench under the banyan trees. Once we have finished eating and talking, we wander into the library to spend the next twenty minutes amongst the various volumes of ancient and new books.

It has become a bit of a ritual now, these lunch meetings. Subhash listens with interest when I tell him about my views about the world right now, and especially my irritation with religion – the way it divides the world. I have even shown him the poem I found in the park in Delhi, the mystical verses I admire so much, although I have never experienced the kind of spirituality they speak of. I also tell Subhash about Maria and her unconventional view of Christianity.

Subhash seems to appreciate these things greatly. He tells me that the poem I found is similar to Sufi poetry and gives me a book of poems by Rumi. I read the poems with awe, not quite believing the intensity of the love the poet feels for his 'Beloved'. Sometimes the poems seem to be directed to God and sometimes they seem to be about a person. I mention this to Subhash.

"The Beloved is always God and they are all about God," Subhash tells me.

"Oh," I say disappointedly. "I thought that sometimes it was about the poet's lover, elevated to a god-like position in his eyes. How can God inspire such human passion?" I ask before adding, "I'm not even sure that God exists."

Subhash doesn't look surprised by my views. "Why shouldn't God inspire human passion?" He asks me. "We are human – how else can we love God except in a human way?"

"So I guess you really believe in God," I say, not answering his questions.

"I feel the presence of God in my life, yes," Subhash says, looking up at the sky. He turns to me and adds,

"Especially in my relationships with the people I love, like my family, friends, soul-mates."

Then he suddenly asks me, "Have you ever been in love with anyone, Laxmi?"

I feel uncomfortable with the intimate nature of the question. "Just once," I mumble.

"Me too," Subhash says with a smile. "But it's not necessary to have someone special in your life in order to be in love with God. God speaks through many different signs: through Nature, patterns, miracles or just through our intuitions. But God does not control our lives, I feel."

Subhash goes on to tell me that he believes we create our own worldly reality through a form of predestined free-will and that this reality is governed by the law of Karma, not by God, although God can be glimpsed in this world play as the powerful, loving and uniting energy behind everything.

"People in India especially like to believe that God controls every aspect of their lives," he tells me. "This is not because of a lack of scientific education – I don't think science disproves the existence of God, it actually supports it."

"So why are people here so much more religious than in the West?" I ask him.

"It's because they see so much suffering around them that they don't want to take responsibility for it. On one hand they speak of Karma, but they don't take karmic responsibility for the society they live in. Instead they blind themselves with rituals they don't understand, hoping God will intervene in their Karma. It makes it easier for them to face all kinds of problems."

Subhash tells me that he thought a lot about his religious beliefs when he was a teenager, hating the rituals he saw performed around him without question. Eventually he decided not to follow any one religion too rigidly because he felt there was no single way to know absolute truth through relative means.

Like Maria, Subhash thinks that knowing God requires a personal journey. I don't know about his view of God, but I certainly agree with him that it's dangerous to subscribe to fundamentalist religious belief systems that are more about power than anything else.

Subhash thinks that if we believe what others tell us is real or important then we lose our own magic, imagination, thought, and creativity, which are our divine reasons for being born and for living on this earth. Although he acknowledges that religions can be dangerous, he says he has a lot of respect for the people who founded those religions or 'the teachers', as he calls them.

His explanation of the role of teachers goes something like this: people like Jesus Christ, Krishna, Confucius, Gautama Buddha and many others came to free people's minds from oppression, but when the teachers left the earth, society lost the true essence of what they had taught. We tried to preserve the teachers' words in scriptures, by creating commandments, rules and religions. Over time, our vision became very limited by this rigid structure, which ironically, was exactly what the teachers were trying to free us from in the first place.

When I challenge Subhash that the 'teachers' seem to contradict each other quite a lot in their explanation of a universal reality, Subhash argues that we've created those contradictions by manipulating the teachings to suit ourselves. He gives the eastern concept of Karma as an example, saying it is similar to the Christian idea that 'you shall reap what you sow' and that you should not judge others unless you are willing to be judged yourself. Subhash also believes in reincarnation and insists it was mentioned in both Judaism and Christianity before political leaders decided to omit references to it out of fear.

I am intrigued by how much Subhash has read and thought about his spiritual beliefs and the way he questions the world. But I sense a contradiction in him, too. He says that rigidity keeps us limited but I've noticed that he practises some religious rituals in quite a rigid way himself. He always has a red dot on his forehead in the morning, which I know is a mark made after Hindu prayer. He also wears a thread around his chest which can be seen through some of his light cotton shirts.

I decide to bring this up with him one afternoon, tentatively asking him why he follows these rituals. He looks at me a little uncomfortably before explaining.

"Some things must be followed by us, even if we do not actually believe in those things." He pauses for a long time, staring into the distance. "We live in a society, which is a collective reality. We have to honour that society, because the world relies on stable societies to keep it going."

I feel the argument rising in my throat, but I hold back. After all, who am I to judge this man and the way he lives his life?

* * *

Increasingly, I find myself thinking about Subhash even when I'm not with him. I find myself seeing his face in my mind's eye, visualising his open smile and light-hearted humour. He has dozens of friends in this town: he keeps his mobile phone on the silent setting because it is constantly buzzing with messages. A lot of people seem to feel attached to him as if he is their own. I think it must be because he makes people feel like they belong. I admire and respect his receptiveness to others and others' receptiveness to him.

Apart from Subhash, the other person I have been thinking more about recently is Nina Srivastava. I didn't expect I would like her much to begin with, but I have found myself interacting with her a lot in the staffroom lately; she seems to come over to me every time I am sitting alone and I have found her company oddly engaging. Having glanced over at some of the philosophy books I'm reading these days, she revealed to me that she is part of a spiritual group called *Radha Pariwaar*. She has asked me to join her for one of their meditations and I have agreed to go with her to the group's next session. It will be a good opportunity to learn more about the different ways in which spirituality is practised in India.

❏❏❏

Chapter 15

I stay back a little later at school one evening to finish off some marking. Afterwards, whilst taking a walk around the school's botanical garden – it's a relatively small patch of land with exotic plants overgrowing on all sides – I notice the Headmaster of the school, Mr Agarwal, taking a quiet walk with a lady dressed in *hijab*, the Islamic dress code. The two are holding hands. The next morning, I mention this to Subhash. He nods knowingly.

"She is a widow. It's a known secret – their relationship," he explains cryptically.

"But why keep it a secret?" I ask. "He's unmarried, so why doesn't he marry her if he loves her?"

Subhash looks at me as though I have said something naïve. "This society would not accept it so easily," he says simply. I don't ask anything more, even though I want to. The bell for class begins to ring.

The girls in my Year Seven class have begun going through changes. I have overheard some of them whispering about it. I heard one of them ask another one, "But why does it happen? It doesn't make sense!" I'm surprised they know so little at their age. It seems some of them didn't know about the menstruation cycle until they began experiencing it.

I feel that, as their teacher, I should be able to offer some guidance or support. I have been thinking about explaining it to them, but it fills me with discomfort and part of me doesn't want to take on the responsibility. Then it occurs to me that there is more than one way to explain something.

After school, I walk into the city where there is a small cyber café. I enter the dingy shop and I walk up the precariously twisted staircase that leads into an even dingier room crammed with computers. An hour later, I have found exactly what I need.

* * *

During my next class with the Year Seven group, I hand out a few printed copies from 'sex education for pre-teens: a dummy's guide'. The girls are agape with interest and embarrassment and I feel quite uncomfortable myself. I sit quietly as they read in groups, whispering and gasping with horror. The simple biological diagrams will give them the explanations they need for what is going on with them. They are unlikely to share this information with their families, who I think may not approve.

There is a chance I will get into trouble for doing this if anyone in the school finds out, but I know I have good reasons for this small digression from teaching English, so I'm not afraid to take a chance in this situation.

The loss of innocence is always so heartbreaking. Childhood innocence and unknowing faith can never be reinstated once they are gone.

* * *

Later on in the day, Subhash and I meet for lunch as usual. We do not discuss anything more about the Headmaster's affair, although Subhash's views on the issue are still bothering me. He seems to sense a tension in the air and there is an awkward silence for a few moments before he speaks to me.

"I know some of my views sound old-fashioned to you," he says awkwardly. "But it's hard for an individual to challenge society so easily. I was just sympathising with Mr Agarwal. I'm sorry if I offended you."

I instantly feel bad for having acted coldly towards Subhash and the tension between us soon begins to fade. I know he means well and he has no real need to apologise to me. We resume our natural flow of conversation, with Subhash telling me about a book he is reading on near-death experiences.

"These experiences confirm the existence of the soul beyond the body, of reincarnation, of Karma, everything," Subhash says emphatically.

"Yes, but they could just be dreams or hallucinations," I remind him.

"They are too profound for that, although dreams are sometimes very deep too," Subhash replies. "Tell me, Laxmi, have you ever experienced anything unexplainable? Something that made you realise there was more than just the material world?"

I think for a moment of all the strange things I've seen and felt, none of them either satisfying or meaningful.

"Yes," I say finally. "As a child I saw a couple of mysterious visions, like sometimes I thought I saw my grandmother, who had just died. Then later I stopped actually seeing strange things, but I started having other experiences. There's this one thing which the doctors call 'sleep paralysis'. My mind stays awake while my body falls asleep, so I feel trapped in the body but separate from it. They say it's a hormonal thing. I also have recurring dreams sometimes."

Subhash looks at me intently and says, "That's quite a lot of things."

"Maybe," I say, "but none of them mean anything. None of them equals the experiences you say you have while meditating." Subhash has told me a few times about how he meditates at sunset and how this makes him feel totally at one with the universe, as if he's 'touching God'.

"But Laxmi, your experiences have the potential to really become something," Subhash argues. "This sleep paralysis, I think if you open your mind, you will be able to change it into a spiritual experience instead of feeling trapped. And your recurring dream is probably some kind of message. I think your scepticism about God and religion is holding you back."

I laugh at Subhash's concerned expression, but some part of his advice makes a lot of sense. I know that the dream is a result of my confusion over my identity. Maybe it's telling me to do more than just get to know my cultural roots. If there is such a thing as a spiritual essence, I think I'm ready to know what it is. I have always seen the physical world as a very limited place and the views of people like Maria and Subhash make me want to find out for myself if anything worthwhile actually exists beyond it or even if whatever exists is reachable for ordinary people like me.

❏❏❏

Chapter 16

The weeks have been flying by like a loose leaf on a strong breeze. I have taken Subhash's words on board and decided to find my own understanding of spirituality. But I need some guidance in this alien territory, which surprisingly, I seem to have found.

I have just come home after attending my third *Radha Pariwaar* group meeting. Nina Srivastava took me to the first one but this is a beginner's class so I'm attending without her now. Six months in Dharna and I've found the town to be generally very conservative, without many avenues for exploring different faiths. The temples, churches and mosques all follow very traditional practices based on scripture and ritual.

In this context, it's refreshing to see *Radha Pariwaar's* attempt at forming a more experience-based spirituality. The group's philosophy is fascinating. They insist that the way human beings are living right now – indulging in self-gratification and ego – has led to misery. They propose a new lifestyle which involves renouncing conventions like marriage and family in an attempt to clean one's inner self and hence clean up the world. The outer is a reflection of the inner, so if you want the outside world to be better, you have to become better within – this makes sense to me.

The group also says you have to stop thinking of yourself as a personality and understand yourself as an eternal soul. You have to give up your own hankerings and understand what is best for the soul. The soul needs peace. Peace cannot be found in attachments to other people and things. Peace means independence from everything external to yourself. Peace means serving the world selflessly, by caring for the world and passing on true knowledge.

I have been deeply drawn in by the group's teachings and for the first time, I have experienced a very deep meditation session with them in which I felt surrounded by light. I think I'm beginning to understand Subhash's experience of a universal connection beyond material reality.

Radha Pariwaar's mission makes sense to me. I have had problems building relationships all my life because

I was afraid of becoming dependent on another person and later being hurt. *Radha Pariwaar* has confirmed that my fears are not unfounded, that there is danger in relationships, and that there is an alternative way of life which does not insist on having conventional relationships.

It's all happened so fast that collecting my thoughts has taken up all my time and so far I haven't told Subhash how much the group has affected me. I am ready to tell him now.

* * *

Subhash is silent and subdued, and when he speaks he does not sound like his usual light-hearted self. I have just told him about my involvement with *Radha Pariwaar*. With a serious look he tells me to be wary of the group.

"The members of that group are not as pure and innocent as you may think. Many of them are fanatics. They use Hindu beliefs to justify an extremist practice which is not part of Hindu philosophy. They encourage husbands and wives to abandon each other in order to follow a 'pure' life, without considering how much damage this does to their families and their children. They preach that sex is the same as lust and they use guilt to enforce their practices. They even try to prey on young children who haven't developed the ability to question or make choices, children as young as six or seven. Laxmi, please don't be influenced by this sect.

If you want to learn about God, follow your heart... read about all the religions and their different mystics. I hope I haven't upset you, but I want you to remain safe and happy, mentally and emotionally. This group is not the way."

It was too much information for me to take in all at once. *Fanatics, extremist, use guilt, prey on children...?* But the group didn't come across like that at all. And what about the wonderful meditation experience I had had?

"But Subhash," I say, "I had a lovely meditation experience in that group, where I felt so free like I was flying. I've never experienced that before."

"Yes, perhaps the group does have some power," Subhash admitted. "But it's not something which will benefit you in the long run. Their beliefs are like taking a drug which manipulates your brain. And if you have the ability to experience this kind of meditation, then it's probably because of who you are, not because of them. You can do it in a safer way yourself. People experience being out of their bodies, having visions, all kinds of mystical phenomena without being part of a sect. In fact, the greatest mystics made their own path and everyone who followed them blindly just held onto something that had already been created by someone else. Groups have a lot of power because they are the consciousness of many people working together, but not all groups are good, Laxmi. I know a lot of people who have lost their inner freedom this way."

I nod but still feel a little confused about what to think. I trust Subhash, but I can't deny what I felt when I was at the group meeting. I know that my ability to experience the deep meditation came partly from me, but the group made it much easier for some reason.

Recently, I have experienced being almost out-of-body on many occasions, but have never quite managed to do it. This happens during my usual spells of sleep paralysis, when the mind wakes up suddenly while the body is still sleeping. I have read that this state of paralysis is experienced by around fifteen percent of the world's population at least once in their lifetimes. I experience this state frequently and I am beginning to doubt the medical explanation that this is all due to an imbalance in sleep hormones.

Feeling trapped in the body is very debilitating during this state until my body regains sensation and I've tried somehow exiting the body a few times now without success. Subhash said that this experience had the potential to turn into something special and I think being part of *Radha Pariwaar* will enable me to finally experience out-of-body travel from within this state.

Whilst working at the bookshop in London, I looked into many books on 'astral projection', which is when a person's consciousness travels through a spiritual realm before coming back to the body which it has a link with. I want to know if this kind of experience is possible for me.

Apart from helping me resolve my sleep paralysis spells, I think the *Radha Pariwaar* meditation sessions could help me to break the cycle of my recurring dream. Then there is also the fact that the group explained my fear of relationships so well: relationships can never give me what I truly need. *Radha Pariwaar* can give me a link with God which makes relationships unnecessary. I mention all this to Subhash. He shakes his head.

"Laxmi, this is exactly how *Radha Pariwaar* uses fear and guilt to keep you tied down to them. You are here on earth in order to experience relationships! Why would God be so possessive? I bet they told you that God wants you to stay away from relationships for your own good, because all relationships will hurt you – this is a clever lie; relationships are not all bad and if you can't make them work, that's a weakness in you and no one else. People who don't want to face the challenges of the world run to hide in places like *Radha Pariwaar*. I don't think you are like one of those people. Many people who have addictions have gone to sects like this for therapy, only to have their addictions replaced by another type of dependency – dependency on the sect and everything it represents."

But Subhash, I think to myself, *maybe I am like one of those people who needs sects like Radha Pariwaar to depend on.*

I don't say anything as the bell for class begins to ring.

* * *

My classes have been running quite smoothly as the children have begun to trust me and respect me. Planning my lessons has also become much easier. I have noticed that asking the children simple questions often leads to rich debates, which shows that their minds are developing very fast.

Over the months, I have had three levels to teach and each level has provided me with challenges and rewards. I didn't think teaching would be so fulfilling, but it has surprised me. Sometimes I do feel very tired, but in general I have adjusted to the rhythm of work at the school and I have also gained a new appreciation of my colleagues.

* * *

One afternoon as I am relaxing in the staffroom after a demanding lesson, Nina Srivastava comes and sits next to me. I look around for Subhash but he is nowhere to be seen.

"So, how did you find our RP group meeting yesterday?" Nina asks curiously.

"Oh, I really enjoyed it," I say. Nina looks pleased. I hesitate for a moment but decide it's best to be frank and go on. "I'm a little concerned though," I say, "because Subhash warned me not to get involved with them."

Nina looks offended and annoyed. "Well, I wouldn't get so attached to Subhash's views if I were you," she says bitterly. "After all, he's getting married in six months and I'm sure he won't be able to give you so many opinions once his wife arrives. Go with your own feelings about *Radha Pariwaar.*"

Nina walks off to talk to some other teachers and leaves me to digest what she has just said. A sudden feeling of hurt and shock overtakes me. The one person I opened up to and shared so much of my deep thoughts with did not think it necessary to tell me something so important about himself – that he is engaged to be married?

❑❑❑

Chapter 17

I have settled into my own rhythm in Dharna and another month has passed very quickly. Questions about *Radha Pariwaar* and Subhash's engagement have been bothering me but I've tried to hold off from thinking about them for the time being, especially as the school is going through its final exams season and there has been a lot of work to do.

I am still going to *Radha Pariwaar's* meetings and it's causing me a lot of confusion because the philosophy, the meditations and the energy in those gatherings are all very powerful; yet, at the same time, their practices really are quite rigid in the way Subhash described.

On Saturday mornings, Subhash and I usually meet for a coffee at Moonpeak Café, which is the only place in Dharna that serves real, frothy cappuccinos made with real ground coffee. Subhash usually brings a newspaper and we discuss our favourite topics: politics, culture, society, literature and spirituality.

This time Subhash has given me yet another book full of Sufi poetry, saying it is to remind me that I can find God on my own, without *Radha Pariwaar*. He says that even the Sufis follow a set path and encourage having a guru-like teacher, but their poems reinforce to him that the ultimate experience of God is personal.

* * *

Later on in the day, I do my weekly shopping at the market and tidy up Mr Chakram's small quarters. It is too hot to sit in the courtyard now. The heat is intensifying in wait of the monsoon. I sit in the living room under the noisy jangling of the old fan and begin reading the volume of poetry.

The sky was lit by the splendour of the moon,

So powerful I fell to the ground -

Your love has made me sure

I am ready to forsake this worldly life and surrender to the magnificence of your Being.

I see that Subhash is trying to show me that a relationship with God is possible in many ways. The Sufis talk about dying to the world and being reborn in connection with

God. Subhash says 'forsaking the world' does not mean trying to escape its challenges; it means letting go of the hold that worldly values have on us, letting go of the false egos we've created in this temporary drama. *Radha Pariwaar's* ideology is actually very similar to this.

The reason the group encourages a certain way of life is in order to help its followers remain strong while facing the pressures of society. Subhash seems to have a real issue with *Radha Pariwaar's* insistence on set practices like a strict diet, celibacy and fewer interactions with what the group calls 'materialistic people'. Subhash thinks we have to make such lifestyle choices by ourselves, not by group pressure through what he says is 'spiritual blackmail' – this involves ideas like *karmic* punishment if a person turns away from the group and the promise of going to heaven for those who follow the group's every word.

I know enough about *Radha Pariwaar* now to be able to see that its leaders do use these forms of blackmail, even with young children who can't debate what they are told. But I'm still finding the group's essential philosophy and meditations very useful in making me rethink my place in the world. I don't like that a lot of people in the group seem to be motivated mainly by the promise of going to heaven in the afterlife, though. If God can be found on this path, then I feel that the love of God should be a reward in itself.

I put down the volume of poetry and turn to Mr Chakram's small shelf of tattered old books to see if there is anything there on spirituality, although it's unlikely. There are a few classic English novels and a book with no name on its spine. I draw it out and find that it is a diary. I open the first page: Sunita Gupta, 1979. This was my mother's name. A bookmark falls out of the diary, marked with a *Radha Pariwaar* rose, the group's symbol. There is nothing more written in the diary.

I know my mother and father lived in this house before their accident, but no one ever told me that my mother was a member of *Radha Pariwaar*. Yet another significant detail about my own family which I did not know.

I walk out into the heavy heat towards Mr Chakram's house and ring his doorbell a couple of times. He answers after a while, looking as though he has been roused from his afternoon nap.

"I'm sorry to disturb you at this time, Mr Chakram, but I need to ask you something very important."

"Come in Laxmi," he says with a tired smile.

We sit in his living room and his housekeeper brings some tea. "Please take," Mr Chakram says kindly. "It is almost 5pm – evening tea time. I hope everything is all right with the house?"

"Thank you. Yes, fine, Mr Chakram. I really want to ask you about something more personal. It's about my family. My mother – was she involved with the spiritual group, *Radha Pariwaar*?"

Mr Chakram begins to look very uncomfortable.

"Laxmi, did your uncle not tell you?" he asks. I shake my head and he sighs.

"Well, I suppose you are grown up now and should know what happened," he begins. "Your father joined *Radha Pariwaar* after marriage while your mother was pregnant with you. They encourage a single, celibate life, you know. Few months after your *janam*, err, birth, your father wanted to leave the family and join them at their retreat centre in Rajasthan. Your mother wanted to discourage him but he was adamant to join them. So your mother said she would also come. Maybe she hoped to change his mind and come back to you and your grandmother soon after. So they made the trip but they never reached the retreat centre. The mountainous journey caused an accident and they both lost their lives."

He stops and looks at me. I stare at him speechless. I feel such a mixture of numbness and confusion that I don't know what to say.

"Thank you, Mr Chakram," I say before getting up to leave without touching the tea.

So, Subhash was right after all. *Radha Pariwaar* had torn my family apart and was the reason my father and mother took the journey that ended their lives, leaving me behind with my grandmother. I realise I can't blame the spiritual group alone – my father's decision to go along with the group, to abandon his young family should be the most hurtful part.

But I never knew my father, never loved him enough to feel cheated. I should feel betrayed by everyone who was involved in the events that left me orphaned, but instead I feel oddly calm as the facts begin to sink in. I walk across the town along the river until night falls and there is not a soul in sight.

* * *

Days, perhaps weeks, have passed and my confusion is subsiding slowly. I am beginning to see that I have not managed to discover the cultural roots I was looking for here in Dharna. Yes, I have learned about the town's ways and rhythms, paid homage to my grandmother's memories in her old house and made friends with the local people. But those things have not made me feel sure of myself as an Indian or as an individual. It's the spiritual battle I've encountered that's revealed the most to me about myself. I have stopped going to *Radha Pariwaar* meetings now, much to the disapproval of its members, including Nina Srivastava. They have warned me that I might face suffering because of this decision to walk away. They don't want to believe that the play of joy and pain is a human experience that can't be escaped by joining a group.

I know that there is a grain of pure, simple truth and power in the group's beliefs, but I can see now that their rigid practices have falsified their core of purity. Subhash has been giving me more books on spirituality and I have been discovering my own way through the maze of paths and religions. I have taken what I understand from the teachings of various faiths and I see that there is a common thread tying all of them together. It seems to me that faith is always a question of identity, of understanding who you really are. There comes a point when a person looks at the body and realises it will definitely die, the way Gautama Buddha realised it so powerfully... and if you feel you can exist without your body, then it becomes necessary to understand who you are without the body.

I've begun to see that without my physical role, I can't belong to a certain race, nationality, profession. Maria had tried to tell me this, but her truth wasn't enough for me – I needed to find my own way, through my own experiences. It seems so clear now: if my physical role on earth is temporary, then how can I belong anywhere on this earth? Nowhere and everywhere become the same thing.

Now I see that there is a blessing in the fact that my physical role in this life was not so rigidly defined for me by a particular community or ancestry, because it has allowed me to understand that those roles could never have lasted anyway. I am gaining a glimpse of what it is that lasts, but it is so unlike the material world that I can't explain it in words, not even to Subhash.

I am finding a connection to what exists beyond the material world, which is revealed through the material world in many subtle ways. I don't know whether to call it the soul, or just a universal energy. I cannot explain it yet, this esoteric awareness – it's something which I am only just beginning to understand and I think this understanding will take a long time to mature.

I had my recurring dream again last week but this time the bearded man did not ask me his usual question. He just looked at me and nodded; my mouth was not gagged. The dream seems to have stopped since then. Recently I also feel I am on the brink of reaching out and touching a universal energy of love whenever I meditate, which I do daily now, on my own, in silence. Perhaps this is God revealing itself ever so gently to a mind that's opening ever so gradually.

Although the Buddha never spoke of God, he said that we should be beware of any opinions that do not come from our direct experience, so he was reluctant to preach about absolute reality because he wanted people to see it for themselves. I don't know if I have had past lives, what my karmic accounts are or if there is a Day of Judgement waiting for me at the end of my physical life.

All I know is that there is an energy supporting the universe and I am part of that energy. I belong to that energy just like everyone and everything else and everything done in awareness of that energy leads to life, to fulfilment, to gratitude and to healing. Everything which blocks out that energy leads to darkness, a tunnel that I think we all travel through at some points in this world of oppositions. The inner turmoil I felt, that long tunnel, was necessary to get me here.

Knowing how my parents died has released me from wanting what they couldn't give me – this is how it was meant to be.

My friendship with Subhash is deepening more and more, but he still hasn't told me about his wedding. I keep hinting at it but he hasn't mentioned a word of it. I don't think I'll ever be able to tell him, but I'm pretty sure now that I'm falling in love with him.

❏❏❏

Chapter 18

"**D**o you think you may want to ever settle in India?" Subhash asks one Saturday at Moonpeak Café.

"I will always have this connection with India, but the UK has become my home now," I reply. "I prefer the lifestyle there, so I don't think I'd want to settle here. I can't believe I'll be going back in another month..."

Subhash nods. After an unusually long silence he says, "It is my engagement ceremony next week. You must come."

Finally, the news I'd been waiting to hear.

"Congratulations," I say a little too emphatically. "How come you've never introduced me to your fiancée?"

"Well, you might find it all a bit strange, but I don't really know her that well. It will be an arranged marriage based on caste and background. We only met once and our parents decided everything."

This was not the explanation I was expecting. I thought he was falling in love with someone, even if the match had been made through an arrangement. "But I thought arranged marriages were different these days – you get to date the person before you decide, don't you?" I ask.

"Not in my family," Subhash explains. "My father is a very old-fashioned Brahmin and the girl he has found is even more traditional. I think she would prefer not to have dates; even just friendly meetings like this would be frowned upon. I don't really agree with it but sometimes you have to make compromises for the people you love."

I can't contain my disbelief in Subhash's words, the man who spoke to me so many times about experiencing the truth for yourself and finding your own answers. "Are you serious, Subhash?" I laugh.

Subhash looks very serious. I start talking recklessly and can't seem to stop myself.

"I don't believe you," I say. "You talk about free thought and spiritual expression and you're just as brainwashed as anyone. It's almost as bad as the Headmaster hiding his affair with that Muslim widow that everyone already knows about. Why can't you stand up for what you believe? I don't know how I can respect you now."

I can't quite believe how much I've said. Subhash looks shocked.

"I'm sorry you feel that way, but we can't all live out our romantic fantasies," he finally says quietly.

"It doesn't matter," I say. "I'm leaving for Delhi in a couple of weeks so my judgements won't bother you for long – sorry I said too much."

For the first time in my relationship with Subhash, there is an uncomfortable silence between us that is filled with negative energy.

"No issue," he says in a subdued voice.

The rest of our meeting is very strained and artificial. I feel a sense of regret that my time with Subhash, after everything it has revealed to me, is coming to an end like this.

Chapter 19

School exams are over now, the results have come in and the academic year has ended. The children have done well in their year groups, all passing onto the next level. I have wished them farewell, surprised at how much I will miss them.

Two weeks have passed since my last conversation with Subhash. I have been avoiding him ever since then, which has been quite easy, now that the school holidays have begun. He has come to the house a couple of times, but I have refrained from answering the door. I don't feel ready to give him my blessings to spend his life with someone he doesn't love, but I don't want to hurt his feelings again either.

I feel very disappointed at the situation as a whole. My identity issues have dissipated into a growing self-awareness, so I should feel happy. But the fact that the person I respected so much is trapped by the same issues that he helped me become free from is very upsetting. He helped me see that societal classifications do not define me, that I have a deeper identity which exists independently from society, culture and nationality.

He helped me see that there might be something everlasting in me which transcends everything in the material world. All of this has helped me embrace the material world for what it is, whilst knowing it doesn't define me. And now I find out that man who seemed so wise is trapped by societal pressures himself... I don't want to think of Subhash as a hypocrite. I love him and resent him at the same time.

* * *

As I am waiting at the bus stand for the long journey that will take me back to Delhi, and a week later back to London, I try to put myself in Subhash's situation. I imagine being raised in a traditional Hindu family here in India, wanting to challenge the customs my loved ones have held onto for centuries without question.

I imagine the attachment I have to my parents and the discomfort I feel in opposing their beliefs. I imagine feeling such a strong sense of obligation that it makes me compromise my dreams to live out my parents' expectations. In this way, I begin to see Subhash in a new light: as a vulnerable human being who is learning about himself, just like me, rather than as a teacher or a guide. I am suddenly filled with compassion for him.

I can't help wondering what he might say if I tell him how I feel, if I tell him I love him. But he has already told me about his commitments to his family, and even if there is a chance of anything happening between us, I am planning to go back to the UK soon. I don't think Subhash could abandon his commitments to his family, his town and his country by coming with me, so there isn't much likelihood of our relationship working out in the future. I will just have to be thankful for what existed between us for this short time and try to say goodbye to yet another person I have loved.

The way I have loved Subhash is different to anything I have ever felt before. I think the core feeling always has the same quality, but this time its manifestation is based on a meeting of mind and heart, which is something very new for me. It seems like I have found a connection that could work on every level: the mental, emotional, physical and spiritual. But the person I have this connection with is not ready to be with me and I have to accept that.

It's just the feeling of regret that won't leave me. I did not say so much as a thank you to Subhash for all the times he looked out for me. He did that purely out of the kindness of his heart, not needing to befriend a stranger. I feel sad about his difficult situation, which he told me about with so much honesty.

"We can't all live out our romantic fantasies," he had said gravely. I hadn't tried helping him, encouraging him or asking him about his situation and how he really felt. Instead, I had rebuked his cowardice, which seems so ironic coming from me – someone who couldn't put her own issues aside for another person.

The bus arrives, and as I climb into it, I feel like I am leaving home. I suddenly don't want to leave Dharna – I realise I want to stay here and settle here, despite what I said to Subhash. In fact, I feel like I can make a home for myself anywhere in the world now, as long as there are people around whom I can connect with, people for me to love.

I begin writing a letter to Subhash.

Dearest Subhash,

I want to say sorry and thank you. Sorry for the things I said in our last conversation and thank you for everything you've helped me to see. I understand what your obligations to your parents must be.

I have enjoyed every moment of our friendship over the last nine months or so. You have a beautiful mind which, like a deep river, reflects light onto the world around, but beneath the surface harbours many insights of its own. I truly admire you, and I might as well admit now that I have come to love you.

I wish you the very best in everything you do.

Yours,

Laxmi

I fold the letter and put it into my bag. The bus starts on its journey back to Delhi.

❑❑❑

Chapter *20*

I have been in Delhi for a week now, harbouring the same mixed emotions as my last day in Dharna: contentment with my identity, confidence in who I am, and regret at losing a dear friend, which is a big loss when you've ever had only two real friends. The door to the past – revealing my parents' death, memories of my grandmother, my relationship with Adam – has been opened for me just by being here in India. I have managed to finally accept everything that happened and let it go now once and for all.

My entire time in Delhi has been spent answering my aunt's questions about Dharna and reminiscing about my students, the town, and most of all, my conversations with Subhash. I think of him every time I open the beautiful book of Sufi verses he gave me.

My spiritual experiences have unfolded to a new level. I have been trying to meditate a little every day, and the other night, during one of my sleep paralysis spells, I was actually able to leave the body for the very first time... I flew straight out of it and towards a golden globe of light. I asked the light a question that's been bothering me a lot recently: "What is my path?"

The light gave a very simple answer: "There are many paths but there is only one destination. And it is a *nameless place.*"

After that message, I felt strangely at peace within myself, ready to find my own way through the mystery of each day and also ready to let go of Subhash once and for all. The memories of Dharna and Subhash are enough for me – I don't need anything more from them. I posted the letter I wrote to Subhash at the bus stand because I felt he should know that I had appreciated and loved him. I don't know if or when he'll read the letter, as my aunt has told me on various occasions that the Indian postal service is very unreliable.

My bags are packed to leave for the airport in another hour. The driver is waiting outside the gate. I can see him wiping the car clean with a sense of purpose; he is surrounded by pink blossoms which have been given a new colour in the recent monsoon. I sigh to myself and pack the tattered notepad I've filled up into my rucksack. Looking out of the mesh windows, I see the sun has streaked the sky red as it moves down towards the horizon.

Just then I notice a figure approaching the driver and asking him something. The driver points towards the house and someone enters the gate. In disbelief, I see that it is Subhash, holding a letter in his hand – my letter, written on the distinct yellow paper from my notepad. My heart jumps in my chest as I suddenly begin feeling very hot. The doorbell rings. My aunt is resting in her room so I head to the door and turn the lock with shaking fingers. I find myself staring into the deep brown eyes I have grown to admire so much. They are smiling.

"I'm sorry I disappointed you, Laxmi," Subhash says through the grilled outer door. "Will you give me a chance to prove that I can live by my beliefs?"

I nod and let him in, pleasurably surprised by his arms enfolding around me.

❑❑❑

Epilogue

I went to London after all because I had a few things left to do there and I wanted to see Maria again. But then I came back to Dharna, to be with Subhash. His family members accepted his need to modify tradition and they accepted me as a part of his life. They did not want to lose him over conventions; their love for him turned out to be much deeper than he'd given them credit for.

My trip to India had changed my life. Everything that changed on the outside happened because something changed first on the inside. A thought in Regent's Park prompted a chain of events. I had always believed that the outer world – my name, my colour, my parents – made me who I was.

I realised that these things had very little substance. I saw that it was my own power which had created everything, down to my relationships and my entire experience of life. I realised that my inner choices as a conscious being determined whether I was happy or sad, peaceful or restless, strong or weak. This identity also created and shaped my relationships.

Subhash entered my life when I was ready to accept him and when I felt worthy enough to be with him.

Apart from the fact that Subhash helped me to see myself fully, he also helped me to see the falseness that surrounds fundamentalist beliefs. Rigid groups use something pure and spiritual to cajole people into political control systems. Instead of freeing people's minds, these groups make people more closed-minded and divided. I suppose this is bound to happen because knowledge and ignorance live side by side in this world. That is why it is best to trust in one's own experience rather than anyone else's.

In my experience, the most revealing lesson has been this: *human pain is a natural part of human growth.* Maria always speaks of Jesus suffering throughout his life and the 'cross' which we each bear in an attempt to search for what is true. Leaders like Mahatma Gandhi and the Buddha are also known to have accepted physical and mental afflictions in order to achieve their aims.

I am beginning to understand Maria's beliefs, although the path I have chosen is different from hers and I understand human suffering in a slightly different way. I feel we all go through difficulties in life when we want to reach for something more meaningful, but what makes this pain worthwhile is that it is temporary and its purpose is to experience our highest vision of ourselves.

For me, the journey from intense darkness to profound light has really been about going from a limited awareness of who I am into an awareness of universal love, which I am always connected to if I choose to be. That is the beauty of free-will, which I think works within the context of *karmic pre-destination* – so we always have a degree of choice, no matter what the circumstances are.

I don't like to speak about my views on God because it's such a personal understanding that's unique to each person, but perhaps the only way I can describe my growing belief in God is simply by acknowledging God as the power of universal love. To tune into that energy of power and love, I think we have to live consciously, because so many things in this world are trying to oppress us into a life of unconsciousness and ignorance:

war, violence, hatred, discrimination, fear. It's in the battle to free ourselves from these untrue, fickle forces that we encounter darkness, but it's important not to lose hope that the light exists, that we can come through our difficulties in order to create something much more worthwhile. When enough people realise this and make changes in their individual lives, I honestly think the world can change for the better.

I've found that altered states of consciousness like those induced through meditation and self-hypnosis – or even traditional, ritual practices done with understanding – can help me to keep my larger perspective intact, so I become less susceptible to the negative forces in this world, which are there in all of us, all to contend with as a natural part of the human experience.

Through my relationship with Subhash, I have been able to share my growing insights into who I really am and I have also learned to balance spiritual belief with being in the physical world. The physical world is full of chaos and contradiction, but I'm not afraid of facing anything anymore, because I know I can deal with it. The *Bhagavad Gita* says that the soul is imperishable no matter what we are subjected to, and the *Bible* says that we reap whatever we sow. I have felt the truth of both of these statements in my experiences. I have travelled out of body and realised that I am not the body. I have witnessed my thoughts and actions having effects and consequences in my life.

The idea of home has plagued me all my life... that monosyllabic word 'home' which sounds like the sacred sound 'Om' that people meditate upon. It used to bother me so much that I couldn't talk about any particular place like it was my own since childhood. But now I feel I know better than most people where my home is – it is a nameless place.

ooo